Clay placed his hand at the small of her back.

She stiffened, as if she found his touch abhorrent.

"You'll have to be a better actress than that," he said from behind her. "If you want people to think we're a couple, then you'd better not tense up whenever I touch you."

Libby whirled around, a spark of anger flashing in her eyes. To his stunned surprise, she coiled an arm around his neck, then anger instantly doused as she gazed lovingly into his eyes. "Don't worry about my acting skills, darling." She trailed a finger down the side of his face, a cool touch that shot an unexpected heat through his body. "That's one thing I do very well."

As quickly as she turned it on, she shut it off. "I'll see you in the morning." She whirled on her heels and left him standing there.

Clay expelled an unsteady breath. She was lethal and he'd have to remember that she was good, very good.

Dear Reader,

I was nineteen years old when I left my home in the Midwest and traveled to New York City, seeking fame and fortune. I had visions of appearing in a Broadway musical and becoming a star. Instead I was offered a job as lead singer in an all-male band, and for a year we worked the East Coast playing in clubs.

Instead of finding fame and fortune, I met my husband and put those dreams away when I married him and began our family. That was a long time ago, but I've always been intrigued by the people in show business. It's that interest that made me decide to set my newest book, *The Bodyguard's Promise,* in Hollywood.

I might not have found fame and fortune on a Broadway stage, but I found my happily-ever-after the day I met my husband. I wish you a happily-ever-after in your life!

Enjoy,

Carla Cassidy

CARLA CASSIDY

THE
BODYGUARD'S
PROMISE

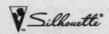
Silhouette®

INTIMATE MOMENTS™

Published by Silhouette Books

America's Publisher of Contemporary Romance

 SILHOUETTE BOOKS

ISBN 0-373-27489-0

THE BODYGUARD'S PROMISE

Visit Silhouette Books at www.eHarlequin.com

Printed in U.S.A.

CARLA CASSIDY

is an award-winning author who has written over fifty books for Silhouette. In 1995, she won Best Silhouette Romance from *Romantic Times BOOKclub* for *Anything for Danny*. In 1998, she also won a Career Achievement Award for Best Innovative Series from *Romantic Times BOOKclub*.

Carla believes the only thing better than curling up with a good book to read is sitting down at the computer with a good story to write. She's looking forward to writing many more books and bringing hours of pleasure to readers.

Chapter 1

"Ms. Bryant will be with you momentarily." The uniformed maid smiled then closed the door, leaving Clay West alone in a living room the size of a small country.

White. White carpeting, white walls and white furniture. Clay wasn't sure if it was the lack of color that hurt his eyes or the fact that he was coming off a two-week job in Las Vegas, a city where nights and days blurred together without distinction.

He jammed his hands into his jeans' pockets and shifted from one foot to the other as he waited for somebody to join him. He'd been hoping that he'd go from Las Vegas back to his home in Cotter Creek, Oklahoma, for a little rest and relaxation.

He'd been at the airport heading home when he'd gotten

the call from his eldest brother, Tanner. Tanner had been short on details, telling him only that he needed to go to the Bryant mansion in Hollywood Hills, that Gracie Bryant, the movie star, was in need of a bodyguard. Gracie's agent had arranged for the protection.

Clay had no idea who Gracie Bryant was or what kind of movies she starred in. He didn't follow the Hollywood scene and the last movie he'd seen had starred a beautiful princess and seven little dwarves. As he recalled he'd made himself sick on candy and popcorn.

He released a weary sigh and moved toward the bank of floor-to-ceiling windows across the back wall of the room and glanced outside.

An Olympic-size pool was just beyond a lush flower garden and a Greek-style gazebo rose up in stately elegance. A tennis court lay just beyond the pool. This private residence had more amenities than the Cotter Creek Community Center. Apparently whoever Gracie Bryant was, she was successful.

He just hoped this case was more pleasant than his most recent, playing bodyguard to an eccentric, obnoxious high roller who thought showering might change his luck. The guy had been a pig and Clay had been grateful that morning when the gig had come to an end.

He turned away from the window, suddenly aware of the sound of a feminine voice drifting in from an adjoining room. He didn't pretend to ignore it, but rather moved several steps closer to the doorway. The best way to be efficient in this kind of a position was to know anything and everything that was going on in the house.

"Charlie, I told you it wasn't necessary." The voice was deep and smoky, but held more than a touch of impatience. "I told you that you were overreacting. Trust me, I'm not happy about this. You should have okayed it with me before you hired anyone."

Clay wasn't sure why, but he had a vision of a middle-aged woman in a severe business suit, a real ball-buster type who had probably never been married and was in charge of running this mansion like a well-oiled piece of machinery.

"You should have told me sooner what you'd done," the voice continued. "He's here now. All right, I'll do it your way, but mama's not happy and you know the old saying."

Clay tensed. It was obvious she'd been talking about him and just as obvious she wasn't pleased he was here. That didn't matter. Clay wasn't here to make anyone happy. He'd been hired to keep somebody safe from harm and that's exactly what he intended to do.

The woman who swept from the adjoining room wasn't middle-aged, nor was she dressed in a business suit. She was clad in a turquoise bikini with a filmy matching cover-up that fell just short of her knees.

Her blond hair was caught at the nape of her neck in a little ponytail thingie and she held a cell phone in her slender fingers.

Gracie Bryant? The woman definitely looked like a movie star. He couldn't help the faint burst of pure lust that kicked him in the pit of his stomach. Even though he never mixed business with pleasure, he'd have to be dead not to appreciate her physical beauty.

He tried not to notice her full breasts and long, shapely legs that were visible through the see-through material of the cover-up, but hell, he was male and it had been a long time since he'd had a chance to indulge in any kind of a relationship.

Her eyes perfectly matched the blue of her swimsuit, but as her gaze met his, he saw a flash of barely suppressed annoyance. She had to have known he'd heard her end of the conversation, but she made no apology or any other indication that she cared that he had heard.

"Mr. West, I presume?" She held out her hand.

"Clay West," he said. Her long fingers were cool, her handshake firm, and he had a feeling this was a woman who was accustomed to getting her own way.

"I'm Libby Bryant." She gestured him toward one of the white sofas. "Please sit. May I get you something to drink?" She headed for the full wet bar in one corner of the spacious room.

"No, thanks. I'm fine." Gingerly, Clay sat on the edge of the sofa, hoping he didn't have anything on the seat of his jeans that might stain the white fabric.

"If I'd known you were coming I would have sent a car to pick you up," she said, and splashed a healthy amount of orange juice into the bottom of a glass.

"A taxi got me here just fine."

Her cell phone rang a musical tune and a tight apologetic smile lifted her lips as she opened it to answer. The smile didn't quite reach her eyes, which remained cool and distant.

"Hello?" The frown that cut across her forehead did nothing to detract from her attractiveness. "No. I told you no before and I'm telling you no again. I decide what she'll do and what she won't do, and until they're willing to come up with more money, the answer will remain no." She closed the phone and set it on the marble-topped counter of the bar.

"Sorry about that," she said as she rejoined Clay, her orange juice in hand as she sat on the opposite end of the sofa. "I understand you just flew in from Las Vegas."

Clay nodded.

She leaned back against the white cushion, her gaze meeting his with a hint of belligerence. "I have to tell you, Clay, this whole thing wasn't my idea. Gracie's agent, Charles Wheeler set it into motion." Those gorgeous eyes of hers flickered over him in assessment. "Are you good at what you do?"

"Very."

She nodded, as if satisfied. "Charlie didn't want to use anyone local. Things are going well and we can't afford any troubling publicity. He told me he worked with your father years ago and remembered he'd left Hollywood and started up some sort of bodyguard business."

"Wild West Protective Services," Clay said. Clay knew his father had come to Hollywood as a young man and had done some stunt work in several films. It was only when Red West had met and married Clay's mother that he'd decided to move back to Oklahoma to start a family and the bodyguard business.

The cell phone rang and she leaped up to retrieve it from the bar, once again flashing Clay an apologetic but tense smile.

"Tell them she's worth ten times that." Her blue eyes flashed with cold calculation. "Listen, Charlie, don't bother me again with this penny-ante stuff. Until you have a reasonable offer, don't waste your time or mine." This time she carried the phone with her and dropped it on the coffee table before sitting once again across from Clay.

"I'm sorry for the interruptions. We're in the process of fielding several offers and things always get tense during negotiations."

"Look, I'm functioning at a disadvantage here," Clay said. "I'm not sure why you need our services. When my brother called me to come out here, he didn't give me any details."

"To be perfectly honest, I think we're overreacting to the whole situation. This sort of thing happens all the time in this industry and nobody gets too excited, but Charlie, Gracie's agent, decided it's better to be safe than sorry."

Libby took a sip of her orange juice and Clay tamped down a growing edge of impatience. He was tired and getting cranky, and he just wanted to know the details of this assignment. He didn't care about negotiations and big deals.

"What situation, Ms. Bryant?"

"Please, make it Libby." She set her empty glass on the

coffee table and stood. She began to pace in front of where Clay sat, moving with sleek, sinewy movements. "Since her last movie, Gracie is on a roll. She's suddenly a hot commodity. We're in the process of finishing her latest movie, there's a couple of commercials to be shot in the next couple of weeks and there's even talk of some endorsement deals."

He suspected Libby was a relative of the successful starlet, maybe a sister serving as a business manager? If Gracie Bryant looked anything like Libby, then she was the epitome of Hollywood's standard of perfect, heart-stopping blond bombshell.

"Anyway," she continued. "At first the letters that came were like the usual fan letters, but in the last couple of weeks they've gotten weird and ugly. I told Charlie that this kind of thing is to be expected with anyone in the public eye, but he insisted better safe than sorry."

So, it would seem that they were dealing with some troubling fan mail and nothing more, he thought. "Have you contacted the local authorities?"

Libby stopped her pacing and Clay breathed a sigh of relief. Watching her, with her long legs and full breasts, walking back and forth in front of him, had been distracting, to say the least.

"Yes. They gave us the usual spiel about being overworked and underpaid. The officer made a report then asked for an autographed photo. I've hired a private investigator to try to find out the source of the letters. What I'd like from you is simply to pretend to be Gracie's friend and keep an eye on her, assure her safety until the investigator gets to the bottom of things."

Clay had a feeling this particular assignment was going to be a piece of cake. If the only thing they were dealing with was a bunch of letters written by an unhinged fan, the odds were in their favor that nothing dangerous would come of it.

"I guess the next step is for me to meet Gracie, then I'll need to see the letters," Clay said.

She nodded. "I'll go get Gracie and I'll have her secretary gather up all the letters we've received to date."

As she left the room Clay stood and breathed a deep sigh of relief. She might not be middle-aged but he had the definite feeling she could be a ball-buster and it was obvious she wasn't particularly pleased he was here. Her problem, not his.

He walked to the window once again and saw a gardener clipping bushes around the fancy gazebo. The area surrounding the house was no less impressive than the house itself. When the taxi had pulled up in front of the security gates Clay had thought the place was a hotel or a museum rather than a private residence.

Palm trees swayed in a faint breeze and near the house several hydrangea bushes exploded in shades of blue and purple.

People didn't live like this in Cotter Creek, Oklahoma. A fierce longing for home filled him. Clay's father's large rambling ranch house was always filled with people. Right about now Smokey, the cook and housekeeper, would be in the kitchen, bustling around to fix the evening meal. Clay's dad would probably be in the garden and at any given time his brothers, sister and his sister-in-law would wander in for a cup of coffee and some chatter.

It had been ages since Clay had spent any real time at home. For the last couple of months, business had boomed and he'd gone from one job to the next without any real downtime in between. There had been no time for women or fun or anything but work.

Hopefully, the investigator who had been hired would discover that the author of the disturbing letters was a housebound, ninety-year-old man who was incapable of following through on any threat he might have penned. And hopefully the investigator would come to that conclusion quickly so that Clay could get home.

"Gracie will be right down," Libby said as she returned to the room. She picked up her glass from the coffee table and went back to the bar. "Sure I can't get you something?" she asked.

"No thanks, I'm fine." He turned his gaze to the door as he heard the sound of approaching footsteps.

A little girl appeared in the doorway. Clay guessed her age to be between seven and eight and she looked like a little fairy princess. Long blond hair framed a heart-shaped face and lively blue eyes gazed at him with friendly curiosity.

There were three things in life Clay wasn't particularly fond of: snakes, storms and children. He smiled politely as the little girl approached where he sat.

"Hello," she said, and smiled prettily. "My name is Gracie, what's your name?"

Gracie? His heart dropped to his feet. This baby girl was Gracie? She was his next assignment? Oh, hell no! No way. He'd call Tanner and get somebody else out here to do this job. This definitely wasn't for him.

"This is Bunny," the little girl said, and for the first time Clay noticed she clutched a raggedy stuffed pink bunny in one arm. "She's my friend."

"She looks like a nice friend," Clay replied. He couldn't wait to get a minute alone to call his brother. He'd never worked with a kid before. Hell, he'd never even spent any time around a kid.

It wasn't that he hated kids, he just hadn't ever given them much thought. He had no nieces or nephews, no children at all in his world.

"My mommy says you're going to be my new friend and you never told me your name." She scooted next to Clay onto the sofa and gazed up at him with eyes the color of the Oklahoma sky. It was instantly clear to Clay what the connection was between Libby and Gracie. Gracie was a miniature carbon copy of Libby.

"Clay. My name is Clay."

"I like that name," she replied. As the little girl once again smiled up at him, Clay felt a sinking feeling in his heart. He wasn't going to call his brother and get another assignment. If somebody was threatening this baby girl with her innocent eyes and pretty little smile, then he was right where he needed to be. Guarding Gracie had just become his new mission.

* * *

Clay West was nothing like what she'd expected. When Charlie had mentioned hiring somebody to keep an eye on Gracie, Libby had assumed it would be another Hollywood type, slick and polished to blend into any social situation.

He definitely wasn't a Hollywood type. Although many men in Hollywood wore jeans, they wore designer brands coupled with expensive shirts, and always looked as if they were a little uncomfortable in the casual clothes.

This man, this cowboy from Oklahoma, wore his jeans as if he'd been born in them. They fit his lean, long legs as if especially made by the best tailor money could buy. His dress shirt, while adequate, strained across broad shoulders she suspected had come through hard work rather than hours in a gym. Dusty cowboy boots rode his feet, boots she thought probably weren't strangers to mud or manure.

But it wasn't his dress that disturbed her. And it wasn't that his hair was dark as night and on the wrong side of a haircut. It was his eyes that bothered her, beautiful green eyes that held a whisper of arrogance, a touch of aloofness and a hint of judgment that made her both wary and defensive.

The living room was huge, but something about his presence made the walls close in. As long as he remembered who was working for whom, they would get along just fine, she thought.

"Mommy, is Mr. Clay a director?" Gracie asked.

Libby smiled at her daughter, her heart expanding with

love. "No, sweetie. He's just a friend who's going to be staying with us for a little while."

"That would be nice," Gracie replied.

A young dark-haired woman flew into the room and stopped abruptly at the sight of them all. "Ah, there you are," she said to Gracie. She smiled at Libby. "Ms. Lillian has arrived for her voice lesson."

"Thank you, Molly." Libby directed her attention to her daughter. "You'd better run along, Gracie. We don't like to keep Ms. Lillian waiting. Besides, Clay and I have some grown-up things to discuss."

"'Bye, Mr. Clay. I'll see you later." Gracie got up from the sofa and ran toward Molly. Before they left the room, she turned to look at Clay once again. "Maybe after dinner tonight we could play Barbies."

Libby might have laughed at the frantic look on his face if she wasn't so concerned with exactly how she was going to deal with the whole situation.

She believed that Charlie had jumped the gun. He had just become Gracie's agent three months ago and Libby suspected he was simply trying to prove his worth.

"I promise you playing with dolls will not be part of your duties," she said once Gracie had left the room.

"Thanks. I don't usually work with kids." He rose from the sofa, looking a bit impatient.

She frowned. "This isn't going to be a problem, is it? I mean, you don't hate kids or anything like that?"

"To be perfectly honest, I've never thought much about kids. But, no, it won't be a problem." He said the words with a decisive firmness and she wondered if he was trying to assure himself or her.

"Good, because my number-one priority is my daughter. Her well-being and happiness is all that matters to me." She thought she saw a flicker of some doubt in his eyes, but it was there only a moment then disappeared.

"For as long as I'm here, we share that common goal."

"Good. Now why don't I show you to your room, then we can meet in the sunroom and I'll show you the letters that prompted Charlie into hiring you."

"Sounds good."

He was apparently a man of few words, she thought as she led him through the foyer where he picked up a suitcase he'd apparently brought with him. She thought about telling him that she could have somebody carry it up for him, but she had a feeling he was a man who was comfortable doing for himself.

She led him up the wide, sweeping stairway that led to the second level where the bedrooms were located. She wished she was dressed more appropriately, but she'd been in the pool only a few minutes before he'd arrived and hadn't had a chance to make it upstairs to change.

"Nice place," he said from behind her.

"Thank you." It was a beautiful house that radiated success and money in a town that revered both. They'd only moved in six months ago so it had yet to really feel like home.

She led him into the bedroom where she'd decided he'd stay for the duration of his job. "This will be your room,"

she said as they entered the large room decorated in
various shades of blue. "Gracie's room is right next door."

He dropped his suitcase on the floor. "I'd like to see her
room."

Gracie's room was the second largest in the house, only
slightly smaller than the master suite where Libby slept.
Gracie's bedroom looked as though it belonged to a fairy
princess. It was all pink and ruffles, and filled with toys
that rarely got played with because Gracie would rather
be acting than anything else in the world.

Libby stood in the doorway and watched while Clay
walked around the room, his brow wrinkled in thought.
The man had shoulders that looked as if they could carry
the weight of the world. His tanned face was all taut lines
and angles. In a town where handsome men were a dime
a dozen, Clay West made most of them look mediocre.

He touched nothing, but seemed to be memorizing everything in the room. There was a calm steadiness to his
movements. He lingered for a long moment at the bank of
windows, checking the locks, then gazing outside.

"Why don't I let you get settled in and I'll meet you in the
sunroom with the letters in about half an hour," she suggested.

He turned and looked at her, his green eyes direct and
intensely focused. "My suitcase is in my room. I'm settled.
Why don't we make it ten minutes?" Although his deep
voice remained pleasant there was an underlying edge of
steel to it.

She thought about holding her ground, then shrugged. "Fine. The sunroom is just off the living room. I'll meet you there in ten minutes."

She hurried toward her bedroom at the end of the hallway. There was no way she was meeting him without first getting out of the swimsuit and into something more appropriate.

As she changed clothes, she wondered how long he'd be in her home, in their lives. She wasn't at all sure she liked him, although he was definitely easy on the eyes.

Of course, Libby hadn't met a man she liked in a long time. She'd once thought herself in love with Gracie's father, but she'd been young and foolish and so eager to get out of her parents' house.

It hadn't taken her long to recognize that he was just another person in her life who hadn't understood her drive and ambition.

Libby had been pregnant when he'd disappeared from her life, telling her he was too young to be a husband, too young to be a father. She'd waited until Gracie was three months old, then had packed her bags and moved to California.

By the time Gracie was two, Libby had committed herself to seeing that Gracie had all the opportunities, all the avenues to reach her dreams that Libby hadn't had.

Yes, the handsome cowboy might be easy on the eyes, but there was something about him that set her on edge. She hoped that once he read the letters Gracie had received, he'd come to the same conclusion that she had; that there was no clear danger and Charlie had over-reacted.

If that happened, then Clay West would go home and leave Libby alone, as she'd been for most of her life and planned to remain.

Chapter 2

Clay glanced at his watch as he headed back down the stairs in search of the sunroom. Five-fifteen. His stomach rumbled and he wondered when he'd get an opportunity to eat something. It had been a long time since he'd had breakfast and there had been no time for lunch.

She'd said the sunroom was off the living room, but before going there he wandered around to get a feel for the lay of the house. As he walked the lower floor, once again he was surprised by the opulence, the luxury of the place.

Little Gracie Bryant must be doing quite well. He wondered how many people she was supporting at the tender age of eight. He'd heard the horror stories of these poor kids who supported family and staff at an age when their only worry should be that rain might keep their play indoors instead of outside.

Not my business, he reminded himself. He was here to do a job, not to make judgments about the lifestyle of the rich and famous.

He stepped into a glass-enclosed room with white rattan furniture and a plethora of plants. Surely this was the sunroom. He sat on one of the chairs at a glass-topped table and glanced at his watch once again. It had taken him six minutes to get to this room. She should be here at any minute.

Leaning back in the chair, he cast his gaze outside onto the lush lawn and gardens. This would be a peaceful place to sit and ponder. As he waited, what he found himself pondering was Libby Bryant.

The woman was hot to look at, but he'd sensed a cold core inside her. She was probably going to be a bitch to work with, but he'd survive the ordeal.

Clay was accustomed to dysfunctional people. In his line of work as a bodyguard he'd pretty much seen it all. He'd seen the best and worst that the human race had to offer. Nothing Libby Bryant could do would surprise him.

He glanced at his watch again and frowned. It had been twelve minutes since they'd agreed to meet in ten. At that moment, he heard footsteps approaching. But it wasn't Libby, rather it was a uniformed maid.

She smiled, a cool, professional gesture. "Ms. Libby wondered if you'd like something cold to drink while you wait for her."

"A glass of iced tea would be nice," he replied, wondering how long Ms. Libby intended to keep him waiting.

The maid nodded and disappeared, only to return a moment later with a tall glass of tea and several wedges of lemon. "Would you care for anything else, Mr. West?" she asked.

Yes, I'd like you to tell Ms. Libby to get her ass down here. "No thanks, I'm fine," he replied.

The maid left him alone and he took a sip of the tea, frowning once again. There was nothing Clay hated more than to be kept waiting. He believed in punctuality and thought tardiness to be the height of rudeness.

In Libby Bryant's case, he had a feeling it might be a control issue. By being late she was subtly maintaining control of him and the situation. Definitely a ball-buster, he thought.

Ten minutes later she entered the sunroom. "I'm sorry to keep you waiting," she said, although no apology rang in her tone. "I had to chase down Maddie Walker, Gracie's secretary, to get the letters from her."

She'd changed clothes. Gone was the bathing suit and cover-up, replaced by navy slacks and a navy- and royal-blue blouse that intensified the color of her eyes. Her hair was loose, falling below her shoulders in shiny waves. Instead of smelling like chlorine and coconuts, the fragrance that wafted from her smelled expensive.

She sat in the chair opposite him and stared down at the bundle of letters she clutched in her hands. "These are copies of the letters. I gave the originals to the private investigator I hired. I'm hoping you'll read these and realize that Gracie's agent has overreacted and there is no danger." When she looked up at him there was absolutely no emotion shining from her eyes.

She pushed the letters across the table toward him, then leaned back and stared out the window over his shoulder. "How many people handled the originals?" he asked.

Her gaze shot to him and a little frown marred the flawless skin of her brow. "I don't know. The mail carrier, Gracie's secretary, her agent, me..." Her voice trailed off.

With all those people handling the letters, it was doubtful that the investigator could lift any usable prints. He reached for the first envelope and noted the post date: May 15th. Almost two months ago.

He pulled out the letter and quickly scanned it.

Dear Gracie,
    I think you should get out of show business. You think you're cute, but you're not. You think you're a little princess, but you're nothing. You might fool some people but you don't fool me. You're a talent-less piece of nothing.

It was signed, "Not A Fan."

There'd been a total of eight letters sent over the course of the past two months. What concerned Clay was that each seemed to be an escalation of emotion, culminating in the last letter.

Dear Gracie,

    Why don't you just die, you little bitch?

It wasn't just the words, a growing anger showed in the handwriting itself. The first letter was neatly written in block letters. The last letter was still in block letters but sloppy and the pen pressed so hard in places it appeared from the copy as if the paper had ripped.

Rage.

He looked at Libby. "I don't think Gracie's agent over-reacted. If Gracie were my daughter, I'd be more than a little concerned about these letters."

She held his gaze for a long moment and in the depth of her eyes he saw a flicker of emotion for the first time. An edge of fear. A whisper of vulnerability. So, the woman had an Achilles' heel, and it was her daughter, apparently.

She swept a hand through her hair, causing it to ripple across her shoulder. "So what do we do now?" she asked, then cleared her throat as if swallowing a lump.

"We keep your daughter safe," he replied. For the first time since he'd arrived he felt as if he had her full, undivided attention. "What I'll need from you is Gracie's daily schedule."

"Done."

"I also need you to make a list of all the people who surround her."

She frowned again. "That's going to be quite a list. Gracie is in the middle of filming a movie. Her schedule is hectic and there's no way I can list everyone who works on the movie set."

"Do the best you can," he replied. "I want teachers, staff, along with everyone she interacts with outside the house. From now until we decide the threat has passed, she won't go anywhere without me."

Libby's frown deepened and she tapped perfectly manicured fingernails on top of the glass table. "This is going to get complicated. We're in negotiations for her next movie role. It's important that the press doesn't get hold of this, that nobody knows we're worried about Gracie's safety."

"Unfortunately there's no way I can be inconspicuous," he said. God forbid they screw up Gracie's next movie deal, he thought with a touch of irritation.

She stopped her finger tapping and leaned back in the chair, her eyes focused once again out the windows. "It's going to look odd, you hanging out everywhere with Gracie. People will wonder who you are and why you're hanging around us."

Clay remained silent, wondering what she was going to come up with to explain his presence. He'd obviously entered a place of illusion, where nothing was as it seemed and appearances were everything.

Her gorgeous blue eyes focused on him once again. "I suppose if anyone asks, we can say you're my boyfriend." Her expression held a touch of distaste, as if she found the very idea rather appalling.

He wasn't too thrilled with the idea, either. She sure as hell wasn't his type of woman. He didn't go for the ice princess types. "You're the boss," he replied.

"We'll tell people we met several months ago at a charity function and have been secretly dating ever since." Her gaze flickered down the length of him. "You're a wealthy retired rancher, and that's all anyone needs to know."

"Won't your friends wonder why you haven't mentioned me before to them?"

"This is Hollywood. I don't have close friends," she replied.

He had a feeling that the fact that she didn't have close friends was less about Hollywood and more about the woman herself. She didn't seem like the type who would give much of herself to anyone. Of course, it was too early for him to form any definite opinions about her.

Her gaze flickered over him once again. "We have a lot going on over the next couple of weeks, events that will require formal dress. I don't suppose you have a tuxedo in that little suitcase of yours." There was a tone in her voice that indicated she doubted he'd ever worn a tux, let alone owned one.

"Unfortunately, when I packed my bags my tux was at the cleaner's," he said dryly.

"I'll have Enrique bring some things over for you from his shop. If you're going to attend the various events with Gracie and me, you need to be dressed appropriately. Don't worry, I'll take care of the cost."

The irritation Clay had been fighting since the moment he'd arrived rose up. "That's not necessary. I can afford to buy my own clothes, even in Hollywood."

She opened her mouth as if to protest, but must have seen something on his face that made her think twice. "Suit yourself," she said. "I'll make the arrangements for sometime tomorrow afternoon with Enrique."

"Where is Gracie now?" he asked.

"Up on the third floor with her voice teacher. There are several rooms up there, including a place where Gracie has her various lessons and works out with her physical trainer."

A physical trainer for an eight-year-old? Once again he realized he was in a world unfamiliar to everything he knew.

"If we're finished here, then I'd like to go up to the third floor and take a look around."

"All right, and I'll see to it that you have a schedule of her daily activities and that list of people by the end of the evening."

She stood, looking as if she'd like nothing better than to escape his presence. "Dinner is served at seven in the dining room. If you need anything else, I'll be in my office getting together those things for you."

Clay stood as she left the sunroom, the scent of her perfume lingering in the air. He'd hoped that when he read the letters he'd be able to tell her there was nothing to worry about and he'd be able to leave la-la land and head back home to Cotter Creek.

But the letters had disturbed him. It was possible they were nothing more than the work of a harmless fanatic, but he wasn't willing to take that chance. He might gamble on other things, but not on a little girl's life.

He left the sunroom and headed for the stairs to the third floor. He'd thought his gig in Las Vegas had been torturous, but he had a feeling that was nothing compared to playing bodyguard to an eight-year-old and pretend boyfriend to a woman he didn't even like very much.

It was almost seven when Libby left her bedroom for dinner. She'd spent the past hour getting the things together for Clay and trying not to let thoughts of the man distract her from the job.

Something about him put her on edge as nobody had in a very long time. She'd called Charlie, Gracie's agent, to find out more about Clay West. What he'd told her had surprised her.

Wild West Protective Services, the family business Clay worked for, was a million-dollar industry owned by Red West, Clay's father. When Clay had said he could afford to pay for his own clothing, according to Charlie, he wasn't lying.

Not that she cared about how much money he might have in his bank account. She just wanted him to handle the issue of Gracie's safety. That's all she wanted from the tall, handsome cowboy.

She frowned as she thought about having to pretend that he was her current love interest. It certainly wasn't her ideal scenario, but it would have to do. If anyone knew about the threat against Gracie, it could screw up the negotiations for her next film, among other things.

In this case, any publicity wasn't better than bad publicity. Any director would say that children were difficult enough to work with without extenuating circumstances.

Gracie met her in the hallway, a bright smile decorating her pretty little face. While Libby had worked in her office, Gracie had been busy, as well. She'd not only had her voice lesson, but that had been followed by a half hour of schoolwork with her tutor.

"I'm starving," Gracie proclaimed. Clay appeared just behind her. "And Mr. Clay is starving, too."

"Then I guess we'd better get downstairs and see what's for dinner," Libby said. As she walked with Gracie down the stairs, she was acutely conscious of Clay just behind them.

"Mr. Clay said he hoped we weren't vegetarians," Gracie continued. "I didn't know what that meant and he explained it to me. I told him you make me eat vegetables, but we have meat, too."

They left the stairs and walked into the large dining room where three places were set at one end of the long table. Libby sat where she always did, at the head of the table. Gracie sat on her left and she motioned Clay into the chair at her right.

They had just seated themselves when the cook, Helen Richmond, served the first course. A bowl of soup.

"Helen, this is Clay West. He's going to be my guest for a while," Libby said.

Clay nodded at the plump, white-haired woman. "Nice to meet you, Helen."

She gave him a curt nod, then disappeared into the

kitchen. Helen was an ill-tempered beast most of the time, but she had a reputation as one of the best cooks in Hollywood. It had been a real coup when Libby had managed to hire her.

"Mr. Clay has a cook. His name is Smokey," Gracie said as they began to eat. "Mr. Clay says he's grouchy." She smiled at Libby. "Kind of like Ms. Helen, right, Mom?"

"That's not nice, Gracie," Libby chided.

Gracie shrugged. "But it's true."

Libby couldn't help biting back a smile. If there was one thing she'd learned about her daughter, it was that Gracie was surprisingly opinionated for her age.

"You have any brothers or sisters, Clay?" she asked. She'd prefer meaningless small talk to silence.

"Four brothers, one sister."

"I wish I had a sister or a brother," Gracie said. "Definitely a sister, I'd have to think about a brother. Jennifer's little brother is a big pain." She looked at Clay. "Are your brothers big pains?"

He looked at Gracie and a smile curved his lips, the first smile Libby had seen on his face. The attractiveness of it hit her in the pit of the stomach like a small kick.

"Brothers can definitely be big pains, but they can also be the best friends you'll ever have in your life," he said.

"My best friend's name is Kathryn. She's a girl," Gracie said. "She's an actress, too, and I get to see her every day on the set."

"Is she your age?" Clay asked.

"No, she's a year older than me. She has a birthday

coming up and she's going to be nine. She thinks she's much smarter than me because she'll be nine before I will be." Gracie released a long-suffering sigh. "She's kind of a know-it-all, but she's my best friend anyway."

At that moment Helen returned to take away the soup dishes and to serve the main course of Swiss steak, baked potato and fresh, steamed asparagus.

Thankfully, Clay offered nothing more personal about himself throughout the course of the meal. Libby didn't want to know anything personal about him. It was enough that he had a killer smile. It was enough that he bothered her on a level she didn't quite understand.

Gracie kept up a running monologue throughout the meal, telling Clay all about the movie they were in the middle of shooting, about the other child actors who were in the film and how much fun they had on the set.

Although Clay wasn't big on conversation, he listened with interest to everything Gracie said and it was apparent that in the few brief hours of the early evening the handsome cowboy and her daughter had begun to form a relationship.

Gracie liked him. It was obvious in her easy chatter, in the way she smiled at him so frequently. Libby wasn't sure how to feel about it. On the one hand she hated to see her daughter forming any kind of attachment to a man who wouldn't be long in her life. On the other hand she knew it was important that Gracie trust Clay. Her very life might depend on that trust.

The meal passed without too many awkward silences,

thanks to Gracie. After dinner, Libby told Clay he was officially off duty while she attended to Gracie's bath and bedtime. He disappeared into his bedroom while she and Gracie went into her room so Gracie could take a bath in her mother's tub, as was her habit.

Half an hour later Gracie swam around in the oversize tub. Libby sat in a chair nearby. "I like Mr. Clay," Gracie said. She scooped up a handful of bubbles and put them on top of her head, then posed as if doing a commercial shoot for bubble bath.

"I know. I could tell."

Gracie slid down in the water. "He has nice eyes. They're real green, like grass."

Libby had noticed. His eyes were a beautiful shade of green, but she didn't find them particularly nice. Whenever he gazed at her they were cool and distant and held just the slightest whisper of censure that let her know he didn't think very much of her.

Not that it bothered her. He didn't have to like her. That wasn't his job. And she didn't have to like him. She could find him pleasant to look at without having to like him. Okay, so pleasant seemed too mild a description for the edgy tension that swept through her whenever she looked at him.

"Tell me your lines for tomorrow's shoot," Libby said, hoping to distract her daughter from any more observations about Clay West.

It was eight-thirty when she finally got Gracie tucked into bed and went down to her office for the list and schedule Clay had requested. She'd not only written down the names of the people intimately involved in Gracie's life but also what they did.

She retrieved the papers, then went back up the stairs and knocked on his bedroom door.

When he pulled open the door, her breath caught in her throat. He had obviously taken the time alone to shower for his dark hair was damp and the scent of minty soap wafted from him.

He was shirtless, his chest a broad expanse of tanned, muscled flesh, and his jeans rode precariously low on his slender hips.

Male. The man was so intensely male. God, it had been a long time since she'd enjoyed any kind of a physical relationship with a man. She had an insane impulse to reach out and touch his chest, to thread her fingers through the dark tuft of hair that sprang up in the center.

"Yes?" For just a brief moment his eyes flickered with a hint of amusement, as if he could read her thoughts.

A flash of annoyance shot through her. "I have those things you asked for." She thrust the papers toward him.

He scanned the first sheet quickly, then looked back at her. "I think we need to go over some of this together. In case I have questions or need clarification. Is now convenient?"

Only if you put on a shirt, she thought. "Why don't we meet in my office in a few minutes and go over things?"

"Fine. I'll see you in a few."

Before going back downstairs, Libby went into Gracie's

room to check on her daughter. For a long moment she stood at the side of Gracie's bed, watching her daughter in slumber.

Here was the reason Libby didn't have any personal relationships. Gracie had a dream, a dream like the one Libby had once had.

In Libby's case nobody had helped nurture that dream, but had rather tried to squash it out of her. Her aspirations for herself had been met with not only a lack of support but also a cold censure that had forever broken a piece of Libby's heart.

Like Libby, her daughter had expressed the desire to be in movies, to act. Gracie loved it. Libby had made the decision to forget her own career and become Gracie's biggest support, to nourish her dream in every way possible as nobody had ever done for her.

She leaned down and pressed her lips against Gracie's soft cheek, then turned and left her bedroom. As she headed downstairs to her office, she thought about the handsome stranger who had been brought into their lives.

She couldn't help but admit that something about him was more physically appealing to her than any man had been for a very long time. On screen, it would be called chemistry; off screen, it was just irritating.

If there was any one place in the house where she felt most at home it was in her office just off the living room. The office was large and held not only her beautiful mahogany desk, but also a tasteful burgundy-and-gold love seat and a coffee table.

The walls were covered with framed photos. Some of them were of her when she'd first come to Hollywood and had worked as a model/actress. Others were of both her and Gracie from a shoot they'd done together for baby food, and the rest were of Gracie. They were a pictorial history of their work here in Hollywood that told a story of success.

Whenever Libby wasn't with Gracie she could usually be found here in the office. From her chair at the desk she not only planned and negotiated Gracie's next career move, but also kept detailed financial records and sifted through the social invitations to decide which events she and her daughter would and wouldn't attend.

As she waited for Clay to join her, she tackled a stack of invitations that Maddie Walker, their secretary, had placed on her desk at some point during the day.

They were the usual mixed bag: dinner invitations, several charity events and a surprise birthday party for a director who had worked with Libby on her first film. That picture had been filmed years ago when Gracie was a baby and Libby had been focused on her own career rather than her daughter's.

She tensed as she heard the sound of approaching footsteps. He came into the room, bigger than life and, thankfully, wearing a shirt. He carried the papers she'd given him and for a long moment he stood in the doorway of the room and gazed at the photos on the wall.

"You were an actress?" he finally asked.

She nodded. "I came to Hollywood when Gracie was

three months old. For the first two years of her life I did some modeling and acting." She started to explain to him why she'd stopped working and how Gracie had been discovered, but then realized it was nothing he needed to know.

"Interesting," he said. When he sat on the love seat he significantly dwarfed the overstuffed piece of furniture.

"Did you have a chance to look over the things I gave you?" she asked, wanting to get this little meeting over with as soon as possible.

"Very briefly. I notice that Gracie's schedule is pretty hectic." There was a hint of disapproval evident in his voice.

"Gracie loves what she's doing and she manages the schedule just fine," she replied coolly. How could a small-town cowboy have any idea about the choices she'd made for her daughter, the choices Gracie made for herself?

"What about her father? You don't have him listed anywhere. Where is he?"

"Your guess is as good as mine," she replied.

"So he's not a presence in her life?"

She fought back a bitter laugh. "He wasn't even a presence in the pregnancy."

His green eyes narrowed in thought. "No chance he could be the one sending the letters? That maybe he disapproves of how Gracie is being raised."

"There's nothing wrong with the way Gracie is being raised," she replied defensively. "But no, I can't imagine Raymond sending those letters. If he were going to contact us at all it would probably be for money, not because of some long overdue fatherly concern."

Even after all these years, just thinking about Raymond Willows caused a hard knot of anger and hurt to form in the center of her chest.

He'd been the one man she'd trusted, the one man who had said all the right things at a time when she'd desperately needed to hear them. And they'd been the empty promises of a young man who'd wanted nothing more than to get into her panties.

She dismissed thoughts of the past. The day she had packed her bags and left Middle Creek, Pennsylvania, she'd made a conscious decision to never look back.

"What about boyfriends or lovers of yours? I see you have none listed."

She wasn't sure why, but the heat of a blush warmed her cheeks. "That's because at the current time there are none."

His gaze held hers intently. "No close friends, no boyfriends or lovers. Sounds pretty lonely to me."

"On the contrary, my life is too full for loneliness. Now, are there any other questions you have concerning the schedule or the list of people?"

He glanced back at the papers in his hand. "No, I guess that's it for now, although I'm sure I'll have plenty of other questions in the future."

She picked up a small notepad that was next to the computer mouse and ripped off the top page. "Here is the code number and word for the house security system. And now we're finished here," she replied, hoping he'd take her words as a dismissal.

"Not quite." He placed the papers on the love seat next to him and leaned back, looking every inch as if he belonged. "Now we need to talk about us."

Chapter 3

"Us?" Her big blue eyes widened in alarm. "What do you mean? There's no us to discuss."

"But there is," he countered. "I mean, if I'm going to play the role of your latest boy-toy, then I think we need to get our stories straight."

Again her features settled into the cool, ice princess look. "First of all, at thirty you're far too old to be considered a boy-toy and at twenty-six years old I'm far too young to have a boy-toy."

She'd apparently done some checking into his background to know his age. Twenty-six. Clay did a quick calculation in his head. So, she'd been eighteen when she'd had Gracie. He'd known she was young despite the fact that she had the self-confidence and cool presence of somebody older.

"A has-been at thirty," he said dryly.

"Welcome to Hollywood," she replied, equally as dry. "It's the land of perpetual youth and make-believe."

"If I'm going to be part of your make-believe world, then you have to give me some sort of script to follow. You mentioned earlier that we'd tell people we met at a charity function and we've been seeing each other ever since. But, the devil is in the details. Specifically, what kind of function was it and when exactly did it take place?"

She frowned and flipped through the pages of a calendar on her desktop. "It was a dinner for the advancement and research of childhood diseases and we attended it in the middle of June."

"And one month later we're living together?" He crooked an eyebrow upward.

A tight smile curved her lips. "In Hollywood a month is an eternity when it comes to personal relationships. In any case, that's all anyone needs to know when it comes to you and me. I'm not given to sharing the personal details of my life with anyone."

Why didn't that surprise him? Something about her bugged him and he was rarely bugged by anyone. It intrigued him. *She* intrigued him. Her coolness, the slight edge of brittle defensiveness he felt emanating from her and the wall he sensed she kept erected between herself and anyone else definitely fascinated him.

He stood, deciding that it was time to call it a night. He was beyond exhausted and that was probably why she was getting to him in a way he didn't quite understand.

She stood, as well. "It's vital to me that nobody suspect that you're anything but my boyfriend," she said as they started to leave the office together.

As she stepped in front of him to exit the room first, he placed his hand at the small of her back. She stiffened, as if she found his touch abhorrent.

"I thought you said you'd been an actress. You're going to have to be a better actress than that," he said from behind her. "If you want people to think we're a couple, then you'd better not tense up whenever I happen to touch you."

She whirled around, a spark of anger flashing in her eyes. To his stunned surprise she coiled an arm around his neck, the anger instantly doused as she gazed lovingly into his eyes. "Don't worry about my acting skills, darling." She trailed a finger down the side of his face, a cool touch that shot an unexpected heat through his body. "That's one thing I do very well."

As quickly as she turned it on, she shut it off. She stepped away from him, the flash of anger back in her eyes. "I'll see you in the morning." She twirled on her heels and left him standing there.

Clay expelled an unsteady breath. She was lethal and he'd have to remember that she was good, very good. Good enough to have just earned herself a freaking Academy Award nomination for her little performance.

As he headed up the stairs to the bedroom he would call home for the duration of his stay, he wondered why she wasn't working anymore. Had it just become easier to rest on her daughter's laurels than to work herself?

Certainly, Gracie's talent seemed to be paying off big-time. He frowned as he thought of the little girl's schedule. Work, school, voice and dance lessons, drama coaches and trainers, every minute of every day was filled, with no time for her to just be a kid. It seemed like a heavy load for an eight-year-old to carry just so the adults in her life could live in the lap of luxury.

Before entering his bedroom, he stepped quietly into Gracie's room. While she'd been with her mother preparing for bedtime, Clay had acquainted himself with the house security and had double-checked the windows in the little girl's room to make certain they were locked.

The grounds were surrounded by a high concrete wall and the home security system was one of the best he'd ever seen. He felt fairly confident that while Gracie was inside the house she'd be safe.

He'd also learned from one of the maids that the only staff who stayed overnight in the house was Helen, the cook, who had a small suite of rooms just off the kitchen. The rest of the staff either had their own homes or stayed in staff quarters located in a building at the back of the property. So, he wasn't too concerned with a threat to Gracie coming from within the house itself. Unless Helen hid some maniac tendencies that weren't immediately apparent. He grinned at the very thought. She might be cantankerous, but he doubted she was murderous.

He left Gracie's room, his glance shooting down the hallway toward Libby's bedroom door, which was closed. For just a moment his body remembered the heat of hers

as she'd leaned into him and the sweet curve of her lips
as she'd feigned affection for him.

Ms. Libby Byrant was some piece of work. He had a
feeling she was not just cold, but capable of manipulation
and subterfuge to gain a means to an end. But, damn, she
was pretty.

He dismissed thoughts of Libby as he went into his
bedroom. It took him only minutes to strip down to his
boxers and get into bed.

Exhaustion tugged on every muscle. He'd been on a
whirlwind of work for the past six months. Before Las
Vegas had been Dallas and before Dallas had been a job in
Miami. Job after job, city after city blurred together in his
mind.

When this particular job was over he was looking
forward to some downtime at home in Cotter Creek. Hell,
he hadn't even met his brother Tanner's new wife yet and
they'd been married for two months. In a couple of weeks
his brother Zack was getting married to Katie Sampson,
the young woman from a neighboring ranch.

Maybe he'd be home by then and able to attend the
wedding. As his thoughts turned to home and family, he
found himself thinking of his mother, Elizabeth.

From what Clay's father had told him about his mother,
Hollywood had been her town. She'd been a fast-rising star
before she'd fallen in love with Clay's father, Red. The two
had met when Red had been working as a stuntman on one
of Elizabeth's movies.

Elizabeth had left Hollywood and her career behind to

move with Red to Cotter Creek, Oklahoma, where the two had made a home and begun their family. Clay's oldest brother, Tanner, had been ten when Elizabeth had been killed and Joshua, the youngest sibling, had only been a baby.

She'd gone to town for groceries one evening and when she hadn't returned by the time Red thought she should have, he'd gone looking for her. He'd found her body next to her car on the country road between Cotter Creek proper and the West ranch. She'd been raped and strangled.

Her purse was still in the car, money tucked into the wallet, negating the thought that it might have been a robbery. The murder had never been solved.

Clay had always wondered if somehow her past had come back to haunt her, if some deranged, obsessed fan had found her eleven years after she'd left Hollywood and had killed her. Certainly it had happened before. There were lots of stories of stalking, maiming and murdering of stars by fans.

His last conscious thought before sleep claimed him was that it was his job to make certain that little Gracie Bryant didn't become one of those tragic Hollywood stories that filled the tabloid papers.

He awakened before dawn, as was his custom. By the time he showered and dressed for the day, splashes of the sunrise filled the eastern skies.

According to the schedule Libby had given him, a car would be arriving at seven to take them to the studio where

Gracie was filming her latest movie. That gave Clay a little more than an hour to drink some coffee and study the list of names Libby had provided him.

As he left his bedroom, there was no noise to indicate that anyone else in the house was awake. It wasn't until he hit the bottom step on the staircase and smelled the faint scent of fresh-brewed coffee that he realized there was somebody else up and about.

Helen stood at one of the counters in the huge kitchen, slicing up fresh fruit. She frowned as he came into the room. "If you'll have a seat in the dining room, coffee will be served in just a minute," she said.

"You don't have to serve me," he replied. "Just point me to the cupboard with the cups and I'll pour my own coffee."

She hesitated a moment, then pointed to a nearby cabinet. Clay set his papers down on the countertop, got a cup and poured himself some coffee. As he seated himself on one of the stools at the counter, Helen's frown deepened.

"Guests always sit in the dining room," she said.

"The kitchen is fine with me," he replied. He had a feeling Helen and Smokey, the cook at the West ranch, probably had a lot in common, especially the fact that they were both territorial about their kitchens.

He took a sip of the coffee, eyeing the older woman with curiosity. "Have you been working here long?"

"I've been working for Ms. Libby and Gracie for almost six months," she said.

"It must be interesting, working for a strong woman like Ms. Libby," he observed.

Helen put down the sharp knife she'd been using and glared at him. "If you think you're going to sit here in my kitchen and try to pull information out of me about Ms. Libby, you'd better think again." She picked up the knife, looking as if she'd rather use it on him than on the fuzzy brown kiwi in front of her.

Clay sighed and focused his attention on the papers in front of him. He was still there thirty minutes later when Libby came into the kitchen. Instantly a tension filled the air.

"Good morning," she said to Clay, then directed her gaze to Helen. "Gracie should be down in about ten minutes for breakfast." Helen nodded and Libby once again looked at Clay. "Are you going to join us for breakfast in the dining room?"

"Of course." He got up from the stool and followed her into the dining room, trying not to notice the subtle sway of her hips or the slender curve of her calves beneath the short black skirt she wore.

They had just gotten seated at the table when Gracie whirled into the room. Clad in a pair of yellow shorts and a matching T-shirt, she looked like a little ball of sunshine. The bright smile she offered Clay did nothing to spoil the image.

"Are you going with us to the studio today, Mr. Clay?" she asked as she settled into the chair at the table.

"I am. If that's all right with you?" he replied.

"Oh, yes, it's fine with me. You can meet all my friends and you can see me work. Want to see how I can cry?"

Clay looked at Libby helplessly, unsure how to respond. "Might as well indulge her," Libby said with a wry smile. "She loves to show off."

Gracie stared at Clay with wide blue eyes, eyes that quickly filled with tears. Those tears splashed down her cheeks and her lower lip quivered as if her little heart was breaking.

She laughed then, and wiped the tears from her cheeks. "That was pretend tears," she explained.

At that moment Helen came into the room to begin serving breakfast, and Clay found himself wondering how in the hell with these two females anyone ever knew what was truth and what was pretend.

Maxim Studios, where Gracie's current film, *Revenge of the Kids,* was being filmed was just off Sunset Boulevard. As always, when they passed through the security gates of the movie studio, Libby felt a small thrill tremble through her. She had spent most of her childhood dreaming of the day when a security guard at a movie studio would greet her by name and flag her car through with a welcoming smile.

As they parked and got out of the car to enter the building where Gracie would work for the day, Libby tried to keep her attention focused on Gracie and not on the man who accompanied them. But it was difficult.

He wasn't wearing jeans today, but instead wore a pair

of black dress slacks with a silver-and-black pinstriped dress shirt. He'd looked raw and male in his jeans. He looked hot and utterly male in dress clothes.

Why hadn't Charlie hired somebody who was fifty pounds overweight and balding? Why couldn't he have hired somebody about fifty years old instead of this thirty-year-old man with evocative green eyes and taut six-pack stomach muscles?

"What happens now?" he asked Libby as they entered the building where there seemed to be people and activity everywhere.

"She goes directly to makeup."

"There's so many people around," he said, obviously tense.

"It's a movie set, Clay. It takes a lot of people to make a movie." She still clung to the hope that the threats in the letters would turn out to be nothing, that Clay's presence in their lives was nothing more than an unnecessary precaution.

Besides, surely the person responsible for the horrid letters couldn't be somebody they knew, couldn't be somebody who really knew Gracie. Everyone who knew Gracie loved her. Not only was she incredibly talented, but she had a heart filled with love and a sweet nature that brought smiles to everyone around her.

They followed Gracie into the room where her makeup would be applied. As she sat in the chair and the makeup artist got to work, Clay leaned toward Libby.

"Are all these people's names on the list you made for me?" he whispered so nobody else would be able to hear.

She looked around the busy room and frowned. "Some, but not all of them," she admitted. She wished he'd step back from her. He stood so close she could smell the pleasant clean scent of him, could feel the heat from his body radiating toward her.

"Can you get a complete list of everyone working on the film from the director?"

"I guess I could try, although such a request might bring up difficult questions."

"I have every confidence that a woman of your resolve will think of something," he said smoothly. For some reason he made it sound like a bad thing that she was a strong, determined woman.

He probably liked his women soft and warm and subservient to his big, strong, silent type. He wouldn't find a woman like that in Hollywood. Here it was eat or be eaten. Only the strong survived.

They didn't get an opportunity to talk again until Gracie was on the set and Clay and Libby made their way to a section of chairs designated for the parents of the little actors.

"Libby, dear, tell me where you found this handsome hunk." Delores Gleason, the single mother of six-year-old Malcolm, heaved a sigh that nearly burst her D breasts completely out of their C cups. She held out a hand to Clay. "Please, tell me you have a brother," she exclaimed.

"I've got four, but two are already spoken for," Clay said as he pulled his hand from her grasp. "And those remaining two live a long way from Hollywood."

"Hmmm, too bad. I was just telling my little Malcolm the other day that it was time for Mommy to find a new man, but of course I assured him that he'd always be the number-one little man in Mommy's life. He's going to be a big star, you know. It's just a matter of time."

Libby could almost see Clay's eyes glazing over as Delores extolled the talents of her son. Delores was a bore…a caricature of a pushy, overbearing stage mother.

"We're just waiting for the right vehicle to come along to carry him to stardom." Delores smiled thinly at Libby. "Sooner or later something is going to come along."

"Ah, but right now the movie industry seems to be hot for little girls." Richard Walker joined them and Libby quickly made the introductions. Richard was the father of Gracie's best friend, Kathryn. He was also a single parent.

Libby introduced Clay to the rest of the parents, then it was time to take their seats as the director, Jordan Rutherford, came onto the set to begin the day's work.

Libby still didn't know what she felt about Clay West. Most of the people who came to work for her or for Gracie were overtly eager to please, deferential to the point of being irritating.

In the brief time she'd spent with Clay, he certainly hadn't been particularly deferential. Rather, she had the distinct impression he didn't like her, didn't approve of her lifestyle and couldn't wait to get out of town.

What she found odd was that what people thought of her had never bothered her before, not since she'd left that dreary little town in Pennsylvania. She'd known she'd need to be hard and cold to survive in this world. What she didn't know was why Clay West bothered her in a way nobody had since she'd arrived in Hollywood.

The morning passed quickly. Lunch break came and while Clay sat with Gracie, Libby went in search of Anna Baxter, the director's assistant.

"Anna, could I speak to you for a moment?"

Anna looked like she was somewhere between the age of twelve and fourteen. She was a tiny young woman with gamine features that belied her real age of almost thirty.

"Of course, I can always make time for the mother of our little star." She looked harried and busy, but the smile she offered Libby was genuine.

"I was wondering if there's any way you could get me a list of all the people who are working on the movie." Libby forced a light burst of laughter. "Gracie has it in her head that she wants to start a scrapbook and insists she wants to know the names of everyone who worked on this film."

"Sure, I can probably get a list from payroll. How about I have it for you first thing in the morning?"

"That would be great," Libby replied, relieved that she didn't ask questions about the request but seemed to accept Libby's explanation.

Lunch passed and the workday concluded at two. They were getting ready to leave when the director called to Libby, "I need to talk to you."

A cold dread filled the pit of her stomach. Had her request for the list of people set off some sort of alarm?

Or had somehow word filtered out that Gracie was receiving threats?

"Talk to me about what?" she asked after she'd made the introductions between him and Clay.

Jordan Rutherford smiled and ruffled Gracie's hair affectionately. Rutherford was a big man with a frizzy head of snow-white hair that he wore too long and that gave him an almost demented look. "About our little girl, what else? A script hit my desk yesterday that I think is perfect for her. I'd like to finish up this project and roll right into another with her."

"I don't know, Jordan. We're currently in the preliminary negotiations with Walter Zicar for a new project."

"Screw Zicar," Jordan exclaimed with vehemence. "He's a has-been, an old man who's lost his focus, lost his creativity."

"He won the Oscar for best picture last year," Libby said dryly.

"A crazy fluke," Jordan said, and waved his hands dismissively. "Besides, I'm not talking about an Oscar for best picture, I'm talking about material that will stretch Gracie's dramatic skills and earn her an Oscar for best actress. Wouldn't you like that, little darling?" Again he patted Gracie's head.

Gracie looked at her mother, then nodded vaguely. "You'll have to talk to Charlie," Libby said. "You know he handles all the negotiations for Gracie."

Jordan flashed her a rueful smile. "We both know that's crap. Charlie's just your mouthpiece. If anyone wants to get to Gracie, we all know we have to go through you, not Charlie."

Libby didn't take the time to protest his words since they both knew they were true. "Send me a copy of the script. I'll read it and let you know what I think."

"Done," Jordan replied.

Within minutes of being in the car carrying them home, Gracie fell asleep. She often napped on the thirty-minute ride between the studio and home.

A strained silence stretched taut between Libby and Clay. "Don't forget that I arranged for Enrique to be at the house at four this afternoon to see about your wardrobe. We have a premiere this Saturday night to attend," she said in an effort to break the uncomfortable silence.

He nodded.

"I arranged to get a list of all the people working on the film," she said. "I should have it tomorrow morning."

"Good. Is there someplace I can access the Internet?"

"My computer in my office. Why?"

His impossibly green eyes held her gaze. "My only job is to protect Gracie," he said in a low voice. "I'm not an investigator but I sometimes do a little investigating in order to better protect my client. Once you get that list of names, I want to do a background check into each person to see what secrets I might find out about them."

"I can't imagine that anyone who knows Gracie, anyone who works with her, would want to harm her," Libby replied.

"Spoken like a true mother," he stated. His eyes narrowed

slightly. "If you're smart, you'll view everyone as a potential suspect."

His words troubled her. "What I can't understand is why anyone would want to harm her." She stroked a strand of Gracie's pale blond hair.

"If we knew the why, we'd probably have a better idea of the who," he replied. "Of course, in a case like this it's a little more difficult because there might not be a rational why. If what you believe is true, then some wacko has just focused in on Gracie in some sort of obsessed delusion."

"In which case we might never know who's writing those letters."

Clay frowned, creating a deep etch across his broad forehead. His gaze slid from Libby to the sleeping girl in her lap. "Unfortunately, I have a feeling whoever wrote those letters isn't just going to go away."

His words shot a wave of disquiet through Libby. At that moment, the car pulled up in front of the house.

"Gracie, honey. We're home. It's time to wake up." Libby shook her daughter's shoulder lightly and tried to forget the knot that had formed in her stomach at Clay's words.

"I don't wanna wake up," Gracie said sleepily.

"Come on, honey. We need to go inside."

"I'll get her," Clay said. He got out of the car, then reached in and scooped Gracie up in his arms. Gracie curled her arms around his neck and closed her eyes, obviously perfectly at ease in his strong arms.

Libby got out of the car and watched as the big cowboy

carried her daughter into the house. For just a brief, surprising moment she was struck with a wave of intense longing.

She frowned and consciously willed the strange emotion away. He'd just made her feel crazy vulnerable with his thoughts about whoever was after Gracie.

After all, she had a life most envied. She and Gracie were a Hollywood success story. What else could she possibly want?

Chapter 4

"Mr. Clay rides horses when he's at his house. Can we get a horse, Mommy?" Gracie asked as the three of them shared their evening meal.

It had been four days since Clay had arrived at the house for this assignment. Four days of filming and lessons and bonding with the little girl who was his latest client.

Despite the fact that he'd never had much interest in children before, in spite of the fact he'd never wanted to have anything to do with kids, Gracie Bryant had managed to charm him.

She was so full of life, and possessed a wonderful sense of awe about each day and everything the world had to offer. She was affectionate with him, often grabbing his hand or leaning against him as they walked.

Libby Bryant was a different story. She was beautiful, obviously intelligent and the coldest woman he'd ever met. In the four days he'd spent with her he had yet to get any real feel for the woman beneath the cool facade. She offered no personal information about herself, nor did she request any personal information from him.

Even though it was none of his business how she raised her daughter, his growing feelings for Gracie made it difficult for him to say nothing about the fact that he felt as though the little girl needed a real life.

She needed to have time to play and to get dirty and to sleep in. She should be having picnics in the park and going to a real school with friends instead of supporting dozens of adults by providing a lifestyle of excesses.

"Honey, we can't have a horse. We don't have the facilities to keep one," Libby said. "But on Sunday you'll get to sit on one. Remember you have that photo shoot to advertise Duggin's Dude Ranches."

"A photo shoot?" Clay looked at Libby curiously. She was clad in a silky white blouse and a white pair of slacks with turquoise jewelry that complemented the color of her eyes.

"Gracie is doing a series of print ads for a chain of dude ranches and the first shoot is Sunday on the Hollywood Walk of Fame."

"I get to sit on a horse and wear a cowgirl hat and everything," Gracie exclaimed with excitement. "It's going to be such fun!"

Such fun? No, it was going to be a nightmare, Clay

thought with irritation. What was Libby thinking? Setting up a photo shoot in such a public place? Dammit, was the money from such an endorsement worth her daughter's safety?

He'd been raised that a meal wasn't the time for any kind of a confrontation. Besides, he wanted to discuss the matter alone with Libby where Gracie wouldn't hear him.

"I'd like an opportunity to talk to you later this evening," he said as they got up from the table. "After Gracie is in bed."

She nodded, her cool blue gaze not quite meeting his. He wasn't surprised. Even though they sat side by side every day while Gracie worked, they'd had little other interaction with each other.

He got the feeling that she considered him nothing more than paid help and the lady of the manor didn't mingle with the hired hands.

Ordinarily that wouldn't bother him, but something about this woman bothered him a lot. He sometimes felt her gaze lingering on him but when he'd look at her, her gaze skittered away.

There was no denying that there was an uncomfortable tension between them, a tension he didn't understand. She was so closed in she gave nothing of herself away. Funny, that's what his family had always said about him.

After dinner the usual routine was that Libby and Gracie would disappear upstairs for bedtime preparations and Clay had some free time. He went up to his bedroom and decided it was time to check in with his youngest brother, Joshua.

Joshua was the only sibling who didn't work for the family business of Wild West Protective Services. He'd left Cotter Creek, Oklahoma, and had become a stockbroker in New York City. He'd been remarkably successful and had embraced the New York lifestyle of working hard and playing even harder.

Clay sat on the edge of the bed, unfastened the gun he wore strapped to his ankle and set it on the nightstand, then grabbed his cell phone and punched in Joshua's number.

Joshua answered Clay's call on the second ring. "Hey, brother," Joshua said, obviously pleased at the sound of Clay's voice. "Where are you? Last time we talked you were in Las Vegas."

"California, the land of swimming pools and starlets," Clay replied.

"Lucky you. So who's the client? Some buff-bodied babe with a California tan and a lust for cowboys in her eyes?" Joshua asked.

"Not hardly." Clay laughed. "She's eight, cute as a button and has a lust for chocolate ice cream." He quickly filled Joshua in on the details of his latest assignment. "What about you? How's life in the Big Apple these days?"

"Good, but I'm thinking seriously about going back home to Cotter Creek."

"Why?" Clay asked, shocked by his brother's words. For the past year Joshua had embraced his urban lifestyle and had never voiced a moment of homesickness.

"Something's up back home."

"What do you mean?" Clay stood from the bed and walked to the window, staring outside where night was quickly falling.

"Tanner and Zack seem to think something weird is going on. You know when Katie Sampson's father was killed, murdered by a ranch hand named Sonny Williams?"

Katie lived on the neighboring ranch to the West's place. Clay knew that immediately following her father's death she'd hired Zack to help her find her father's killer and for personal protection. The end result had been the arrest of a ranch hand and Katie and Zack were now engaged.

"I thought that was the end of it," Clay said. "The guilty party was behind bars and that was that."

"You need to check in at home more often," Joshua chided him. "When Williams was arrested, he said the murder wasn't personal, that it was business, made it sound like it was some sort of big conspiracy, but then he refused to say anything more."

"Business? What kind of business includes murder?" Clay asked. "Couldn't Sheriff Ramsey get him to talk more?"

"Unfortunately before Ramsey could get anything else out of him, Sonny hung himself in the jail."

"Jesus. I hadn't heard any of this," Clay replied.

"There's been too many accidents with the ranchers in the area," Joshua continued. "Tanner seems to think something is definitely rotten in Cotter Creek, so I'm thinking maybe it's time to go home."

"I thought you liked big-city life in the fast lane."

"I've charmed all the big-city girls in town. I've decided it's time to go back home and throw some of my charm to the country girls."

Clay laughed. Joshua was definitely the charmer of the family. Handsome as sin and with a smile that everyone found irresistible, as the youngest of the brood he'd been spoiled rotten. "I'm sure Dad and the rest of the gang will be glad to have you back."

"When are you going to be home again?"

"I don't know, whenever this assignment is over," he said. "I'm hoping this particular gig won't last long." He turned away from the window and jumped in surprise as he saw Libby standing in his open doorway. "Listen, I've got to go. Keep me posted on what's going on with you."

He clicked off to end the call and looked at her expectantly. "What's up?"

"I hate to bother you, but it's Gracie." As always when she spoke to him her shoulders were rigidly straight and her words were crisp and clipped.

"What about her?"

"She's insisting you tuck her into bed tonight."

Clay stared at her blankly. "But I don't know anything about tucking kids into bed." The words blurted out of him before he had time to think.

Libby Bryant rarely smiled at him, but she did now, a quicksilver flash of emotion that curved her lips upward and warmed her features. "Trust me, Clay, it's not that difficult."

She turned and headed toward Gracie's room, obviously expecting him to follow her.

Jesus, when she smiled at him like that all kinds of crazy thoughts drifted into his head. Thoughts of how those lips would taste. Thoughts about if she were as cold in bed as she seemed to be out of bed.

He shoved those crazy thoughts out of his head as he followed her into Gracie's room. The little girl, clad in pink-flowered pajamas, was sitting up in the bed, her favorite stuffed pink bunny clutched in one arm. A bright smile lit her features as she saw him.

"Mr. Clay, I think it would be nice if you tucked me in tonight," she exclaimed.

Clay moved to the side of the bed, conscious of Libby standing just inside the doorway. "Honey, I've got to confess, I don't know anything about how to tuck anyone into bed."

Gracie's eyes widened in surprise. "Didn't your mommy ever tuck you into bed at night?"

"'Fraid not," he replied. "My mommy died when I was little."

"That's so sad," Gracie exclaimed. "But it's easy to tuck somebody into bed. You just sit in that chair next to the bed and you tell me a story, then you pull the covers up around my neck and kiss me on the forehead and say, 'Sweet dreams, Gracie.'"

Clay shot a quick glance at Libby, who pressed her lips together tightly, indicating to him she intended to be no help whatsoever. "Can we just skip the story part? I'm afraid I don't know any stories for little girls."

Gracie's lower lip began to quiver and tears filled her eyes. Several tears spilled onto her cheeks. "But you could make one up. I need a story, Mr. Clay. I can't sleep unless I have a story."

Clay lowered himself into the rocking chair next to the bed and eyed her suspiciously. "Are those real tears or pretend?"

Gracie giggled and wiped her cheeks. "Mostly pretend, but I really want a story. You could tell me about being a cowboy." She lay down and yawned.

It would have been easier if Libby hadn't been in the room. As it was, Clay was ridiculously self-conscious as he tried to figure out what an eight-year-old little girl might want to hear about being a cowboy.

"I live in a small town called Cotter Creek," he began, feeling ridiculous. "My family lives on a ranch with lots of horses and cattle."

"I love horses," Gracie said sleepily. "What's your horse's name?"

"My favorite horse is named Amos. He's a big black horse who likes to run hard and fast." Clay began to relax a bit. "Amos loves sugar cubes and every morning when I go to the stable the first thing he does is nuzzle my shirt pocket to see if I've brought him a treat. My father used to tell me that I seemed to like that horse better than I liked most people."

He talked for about ten minutes, telling her about life in general on the ranch and his father's—Red's—big vegetable garden. He told her just a little bit about his brothers and sister, town picnics and celebrations, then he paused and eyed her.

Gracie smiled and her eyes drifted closed. "Now kiss me good-night, Mr. Clay," she said, her voice slurred with impending sleep.

He rose from the chair and bent over to pull the blanket up around her neck. As he leaned down to kiss her good-night on the forehead, he realized that at the end of this assignment the most difficult thing he would do was say goodbye to little Gracie.

"You said at dinner that you wanted to speak to me," Libby said to him as they left Gracie's bedroom.

"I do."

"Why don't we talk in the living room?" she suggested, and started down the stairs.

It had been oddly pleasant to listen to him talking to Gracie. His deep voice had held a hypnotic rhythm and the words he'd spoken had created a picture of a lifestyle that for just a moment was very appealing.

It was easy to imagine him on a big black horse, a cowboy hat pulled down low on his brow as he raced across a green meadow. What was it about cowboys that struck a chord of romantic charm? she wondered as she walked into the living room and directly to the bar.

When he'd leaned down and kissed Gracie on the forehead, Libby had wondered what his lips would feel like on her skin, how they'd taste on her mouth. The thought had shocked her and made her realize again that something about Clay West affected her on a physical level.

"Would you like something to drink?" she asked as she poured herself a glass of wine.

"No. What I'd like is an explanation for what in the hell you think you're doing setting up a photo shoot in a public place for Gracie."

Any charm she'd momentarily entertained for the handsome cowboy disappeared beneath the raw censure in his voice. Before she answered him she carried her glass of wine to the sofa and sat, then motioned him into the chair across from her.

"I didn't just suddenly decide to set up this photo shoot," she said. "This has been set up for months."

He eased down into the chair, a deep frown etching across his brow. "My job would be much easier if we could keep her out of public places."

"That's not reasonable, at least not for this week," Libby replied. "We have the movie premiere tomorrow night, then the photo shoot on Sunday."

"Public places are problematic." There was darkness in his eyes, a silent expression of disapproval that wasn't new. She'd seen it often in the four days that he'd been in their home, in their lives.

"I thought you said you were good at what you do."

A flash of annoyance sparked in his eyes. "I am good at what I do, but only in situations where I'm in control."

"And you like to be in control." It was a statement, not a question.

"Always," he replied firmly.

They had that in common. After what seemed like a lifetime of feeling as if she'd had no control, Libby had worked hard to get herself into a position where she could be in control, and she didn't relinquish that control easily.

She took a sip of her wine and set the glass on the coffee table. "Look, I'm not sure how to proceed in all this. Gracie has certain obligations that would be difficult to get out of."

"I'd think if her life was at risk you'd find a way to get her out of any obligations." This time the disapproval was rife in his tone.

Ever since he'd arrived for the job, Libby had been battling with herself on how seriously to take the notes that Gracie had received. His words caused a flutter of apprehension, a wave of weariness to sweep through her.

She got up from the sofa and moved to the French doors to stare outside where night had fallen and only the security lights on the property illuminated the grounds.

Most of the time she handled the stress of her life and Gracie's career well, but there were moments when it was almost overwhelming. This was one of those moments. But, she'd learned well never to show weakness, that in this town a sign of weakness was the kiss of death.

She took a deep breath and turned to face Clay. "This is my problem," she began. "Neither of us really know how real the threat to Gracie is. I mean, it's possible those letters are being written by a little old lady who doesn't think children belong in films. I can't put Gracie's life on hold indefinitely and there's no guarantee any real danger will ever come from this. Some movie stars get these kinds of letters for years with nothing more coming from it."

"And some get shot in their doorway, when they answer the door, by a crazed fan," he replied. He stood. "Ever heard of Rebecca Schaeffer and Robert Bardo?"

"Of course I have," she replied. Rebecca Schaeffer had been an up-and-coming star but her bright future had been cut short by an obsessed fan named Robert Bardo. Bardo had written to her, stalked her, then he'd gotten the address to her apartment. He'd shown up and shot her when she'd answered her door.

"It was front-page news for months, but that was the exception, not the rule in these cases," she replied.

He took several steps toward her, his mouth a grim slash. "And you're willing to gamble your daughter's life on that? What are you afraid of, Libby? That little Gracie might have to take some time off and you might not be able to pay for your hair appointments with some fancy Hollywood beautician or that she might not be able to pay the gardener or the maids who work for you?"

His words infuriated her. He knew nothing about her, nothing about their finances and was making judgment calls about her without any knowledge. She inhaled a deep breath to steady herself, to contain her anger.

"Not that it's any of your business, but Gracie doesn't pay for any of this." She swept her hands to encompass the room. "I pay for it. I pay with money I earned, money I invested." She took another deep breath. "You don't like me very much, do you?"

His gaze was enigmatic as it held hers. "You don't pay me for my opinion of you."

"That's right. I don't. And I don't pay you to make decisions about Gracie. Your job here is to keep her safe. That's it."

He nodded curtly. "Fine. Then I guess we're done here for tonight." He didn't wait for her reply, but turned on his heels and left the room.

When he was gone, Libby sank back on the sofa and picked up her wineglass, hoping the wine would take away the unexpected burst of loneliness, the unusual wave of melancholy that assailed her.

She'd never entertained a moment's doubt about the decisions she made for Gracie until now. She hated the doubts, the feeling of things being out of her control.

For the last six years she'd done everything she could, made each decision with Gracie's future in mind. She'd never cared much what people thought of her as long as she was confident she was doing things in Gracie's best interest.

What she didn't understand now was why a pair of disapproving green eyes bothered her. What she didn't understand was why she cared more than a little bit what Clay West thought of her.

She finished her wine and went upstairs, plagued by doubts. She went into her daughter's room and sat in the chair by the bed.

She would never, ever, do anything to jeopardize Gracie's safety, but what she'd told Clay was the truth. She didn't know how to handle this particular situation. On the one hand, she believed they were in a low-risk situation and one canceled contract would undo everything they had accomplished in the last six years.

Locking Gracie in her room where her safety was assured wasn't an option, especially since there was no way of knowing how long this situation might last.

She refused to allow some nut to dictate the terms of their lives, especially a nut who so far had shown no overt signs of threat.

The best way to handle the situation was to continue life as usual and to do everything they could to minimize any risk to Gracie. The movie premiere the next night should be relatively safe. It was an invitation-only event and security was always provided.

It would be the same thing with the photo shoot on Sunday. Security would be heavy and only the people working on the shoot would be allowed close to Gracie.

There was nothing else unusual on her schedule right now and Libby would make certain it remained that way. She would turn down any new offers that came in for any extra work or social activities.

All they had to do was to get through this weekend with the extra activities, then they'd go back to Gracie just working on the film set where Libby felt sure she was safe.

She sat for another few minutes, smelling the sweet little-girl scent of her daughter as a fierce wave of protectiveness rose up inside her.

Was she making a mistake in not taking those letters seriously enough? God, she hoped not.

As she left the bedroom to go into her own room, her thoughts returned to Clay. Each time she saw him interacting with Gracie, a longing welled up inside Libby, a longing she didn't understand.

As they'd sat side by side each day watching Gracie work, she'd been acutely conscious of him not as Gracie's protector but as a man who stirred a want in her.

For some reason the handsome cowboy made her think of all the things she'd been without for so very long, like hot lingering kisses and slow, heated caresses. He reminded her that she was a young woman who hadn't known a man's touch for almost six years. Six years ago when Gracie had been two, Libby had indulged in a brief, tumultuous affair with a young actor.

The relationship had lasted a little over three months and had ended when Libby had discovered he'd fallen into one of the traps of Hollywood and liked cocaine almost as much as he liked her.

In the six years since that relationship had ended, Libby had never experienced a moment of longing, a second of need for a man's arms around her, a man's lips on hers.

Until now.

Just her luck that she would feel physical desire for a man who didn't approve of her, a man who didn't appear to even like her. Not that it mattered what he thought of her. She certainly didn't intend to do anything about the feelings he evoked in her.

The last thing she wanted to do was to become a Hollywood cliché, one of those women who slept with their tennis coach, their personal trainer or, in this case, the body-guard.

As unsettled as everything was at the moment, there was one thing that was clear to her. At the end of the day the handsome cowboy would go back to riding the range and she and Gracie would go on with their lives here in the movie capital of the world.

Chapter 5

Clay stood in front of the dresser mirror and checked his reflection. The black tux fit him perfectly, as it should for the exorbitant price he'd paid for it. He was pleased to see that nobody looking at him would know that beneath the slacks he wore an ankle holster that held his gun.

He checked his watch and saw that it was almost seven. Libby had told him that morning that the car would arrive at seven to pick them up for the premiere.

He'd seen little of her or Gracie that day. Since it was Saturday, there had been no filming. Gracie had spent the morning with a drama coach and the afternoon playing in her room. Immediately following an early dinner, Libby and Gracie had disappeared into Libby's room to prepare for the premiere.

Clay went downstairs to the living room to wait for them. He sat on the sofa and checked his watch once again. While Libby and Gracie had been busy with their own things, he'd spent the late afternoon and early evening on the Internet checking what he could find out about the people working as Libby's employees and on the film.

It had been a daunting task by sheer numbers alone. He'd barely made a dent in the list. With those people he'd checked, he'd discovered no red flags, nothing troubling in the backgrounds.

Libby had mentioned at dinner that the private investigator had called, reporting that he'd been unable to discover who had sent the letters. Clay hadn't expected anything different.

To say that things had been chilly with Libby that day was an understatement. In the brief time they'd spent together, it had been obvious she was harboring a grudge over their heated conversation of the night before.

It hadn't been his intention to cause her grief, but he had to do what he thought was in the best interest of his client, and his client was Gracie.

He heard the sound of running footsteps, then Gracie flew into the living room. She looked as pretty as a picture in an ankle-length pink dress, with her thick long hair a cascade of curls.

"Don't I look pretty, Mr. Clay?" She sidled up to him and gazed up at him with her pretty, innocent eyes.

"You look like a little fairy princess," he replied.

"And you look like a handsome prince," she said.

Clay laughed. This was definitely a first, that somebody thought he looked like a handsome prince. He looked up to see Libby standing in the doorway and his laughter caught in his throat.

She wore a scarlet dress that clung to every curve and exposed just a hint of creamy cleavage. The dress fell to her knees and her legs looked sleek and sexy, ending in a pair of strappy red high heels.

Her pale blond hair was swept up in an elaborate twist that unveiled the graceful column of her neck. Desire punched him in the gut as he stood.

"The car should be arriving any minute," she said. For just a moment her gaze held his and he thought he saw a whisper of his desire reflected in the depths of her eyes.

"Mommy, doesn't Mr. Clay look like a handsome prince?" Gracie asked.

"He looks very nice," Libby replied without looking at him again.

The phone rang and Libby walked over to answer it. "Thank you," she said into the receiver, then hung up. "The car is here."

Minutes later, ensconced in the back of the limo, Gracie told Clay about the movie they were going to see. "It's a cartoon about a frog named Freddy," she said. "Do you like cartoons, Mr. Clay?"

"Sure, doesn't everybody?" he answered. He tried to ignore the scent of Libby that filled the interior of the car. It was a crisp, clean scent with a hint of mystery that was incredibly appealing.

He looked at Libby. "Tell me how this works. I've never been to a premiere before."

"As premieres go, this one is relatively low-key and should pull a smaller crowd. The car will pull up out front. The press will be there and as we walk into the theater they'll take pictures and try to get an interview."

"What about onlookers?"

"The general public will be roped off from the walkway and security will make sure they stay back. The security at these things is usually pretty good."

"Good. We'll keep her between us as we walk in and we won't stop to pose for photos or interviews," he said.

"It's an invitation-only event, so there will only be industry people inside."

Clay nodded and tried not to focus on her shapely legs and how hot she looked in the little red dress. In the time that he'd been in her employ, other than the first day when he'd seen her in her bathing suit, she'd always dressed conservatively.

There was little conservative about the dress she now wore. She looked sexy as hell and it wasn't just the outfit. The lipstick that colored her sensual lips matched the gown and seemed to beg for a kiss.

He took a deep breath and directed his attention out the window, trying to get control of his unwelcomed response to her appearance. The tux that had fit him so well when he'd put it on suddenly felt too tight, too confining and definitely too warm.

He needed to keep focused on the job, and the job

wasn't fantasizing about kissing that flaming red lipstick off Libby's inviting mouth, but rather making sure that nobody hurt little Gracie.

As they approached the theater, the limo fell into line behind several others. Clay frowned as he saw the crowd gathered on either side of the red carpet that led into the theater front doors.

If this was a small premiere, he hoped like hell Libby didn't schedule attending any big ones for her daughter anytime in the near future.

When it was their turn to depart from the limo, Clay got out first. Gracie got out after him and, amid camera flashes, Clay kept her tight against him while Libby left the limo.

"Gracie! Over here!"

"How about a smile, Gracie?"

"Say a word to your fans!"

As they walked the carpet, voices called out from all sides. Although Libby and Clay hurried the little girl along, Gracie smiled and waved at the crowd like a true professional.

Clay didn't breathe easily until they got inside and even then he didn't relax his vigil. People filled the lobby of the theater, people he didn't know, people he didn't trust.

He was grateful Libby didn't protest as he kept a hand firmly on Gracie's shoulder, making certain the little one stayed close to him as she and Libby greeted people they knew.

Clay had never seen so many real jewels, fake breasts

and equally fake smiles in one room. He tensed as he saw a big man barreling through the crowd toward them.

Still holding on to Gracie with one hand, he grabbed Libby's hand with the other and pulled her closer. "Who's that coming toward us?" he whispered into her ear.

"The man who hired you," she managed to get out before the man stood in front of them.

"Charlie Wheeler," he said to Clay, and held out a hand. "Gracie's agent."

"Clay West." He released Libby's hand to shake with the big man. "Nice to meet you."

Charlie nodded, then smiled at Libby and Gracie. "How are my girls doing? Libby, you look ravishing as always."

"Don't I look like a fairy princess, Uncle Charlie?" Gracie asked.

"You do, indeed," Charlie replied, then looked at Clay once again. "I worked with your father years ago on a film. I started out in the business as a stuntman, but after several years of getting banged up and brutalized I decided I liked the business end rather than the action end. How's your dad doing?"

"He's doing well. He's kind of semiretired from the family business and is just enjoying life."

"Good, that's good to hear. Hell of a thing about your mother," Charlie said with a shake of his head. "Terrible tragedy. I remember reading about it in the papers at the time it happened."

"It was a long time ago," Clay said, aware of Gracie

fidgeting impatiently. "I guess we'd better find our seats before the film gets under way."

Charlie nodded. "It was nice meeting you. I'm glad you're here for my girls. Drop by the office sometime and I'll see if I can dig up some photos of your dad and me when we were young bucks."

They all murmured goodbye, then Libby, Clay and Gracie went into the theater proper to find the seats they had been assigned.

Clay was grateful that Gracie sat between him and Libby. Not just because of safety issues, but also because he found Libby's appearance and her scent far too distracting.

Once they were seated, another half a dozen people came over to say hello to Libby or to Gracie. Gracie's best friend Kathryn was with her father, Richard, and Delores Gleason dragged a whiny, obviously overtired Malcolm over to say hello. Several of the other children who were in the film with Gracie came over with their parents, then the lights dimmed and the movie began.

Watching a cartoon feature with a child was a novel experience for Clay and he quickly discovered that it was quite pleasant.

The movie was silly, but charming, and his heart warmed each time Gracie giggled with the abandoned laughter of innocent childhood.

Twice he found himself laughing and he looked over Gracie's head to see Libby laughing, as well. He realized it was the first time he'd seen her laugh in all the time he'd been in her home. He leaned sideways slightly in order to hear the sound of her deep, throaty laugh.

Although Gracie certainly seemed to be a happy child, Clay wondered how happy Libby was with her life. She had no friends, no lovers, no life aside from Gracie's work. How could such a lifestyle make any woman happy?

Didn't she want something more for herself, something besides a fancy house and expensive clothes? Was Gracie's success enough for her?

In his thirty years of life, Clay had known more than his share of women, but he'd never known anyone like Libby Bryant. He'd known strong, capable women, but none who didn't want some sort of love, some kind of affection in their life. But Libby seemed to want and need nobody and nothing except her daughter and business in her life.

It was after ten when the movie was over and they were back in the car headed home. Gracie, exhausted from the late hour and activity, fell asleep almost immediately.

As always, an uncomfortable silence built between Clay and Libby. Clay didn't remember the last time a silence had bothered him. He'd never been one of those men who felt the need to chat or to indulge in meaningless small talk. But he now found himself trying to think of something to say to the lovely woman who sat across from him.

"What do you know about Gracie's agent's background?" he asked.

She looked at him in surprise. "Charlie? I know that

he's been around for years and has developed a reputation as one of the movers and shakers of Hollywood. Why?"

"Just wondering if it's possible he could be behind the letters, that maybe he's after a little extra publicity for his client."

Her blue eyes appeared troubled. "I just can't imagine that. Charlie was the first one who warned me that this kind of publicity could be devastating. He's the one who hired you."

"But you're the one who told me this place was one of illusion and pretend," he reminded her. "I've always heard that bad publicity is better than no publicity."

She shook her head and a strand of her pale blond hair broke loose and fell down her neck. He wanted to capture it and feel the silky texture between his fingertips.

"That's true, but I can't imagine Charlie having anything to do with those letters." She eyed him curiously. "He mentioned your mother. What happened to her?"

"She was murdered when I was a kid."

"Oh, Clay. I'm so sorry."

It was the first time he believed the emotion in her voice. Genuine sympathy darkened her eyes. "Thanks, but it was a long time ago."

"Did they catch who did it?"

"No, it's one of the few unsolved murders in Cotter Creek." Clay rarely thought of his mother, who had died when he'd been five years old. He had no memories of her and it was difficult to mourn something you never had.

"How did Charlie hear about it?"

"I imagine it made the papers here. My mother did some acting before she met my father and moved to Cotter Creek."

"Really? Your mother was an actress? Would I have heard of her?"

"I doubt it. From what I've been told she was just at the beginning of her career when she met my father and left Hollywood."

At that moment the car pulled up through the security gates of the house. "No need to wake her," Clay said, and gestured to the sleeping Gracie. "I'll just carry her inside."

"After I get her into bed, would you like to join me for a drink in the living room?"

Her invitation surprised him. It was the first time since he'd been in her home that she'd sought his company alone. "All right," he agreed as the car came to a halt by the front door.

Even though the invitation had only been for a drink, he couldn't help but think once again about kissing that red lipstick right off her mouth.

Libby walked down the stairs after getting Gracie changed into pajamas and putting her to bed. Clay stood at the bank of windows in the living room, his back to her as she paused just inside the doorway.

Gracie had been right. Clad in the tuxedo, Clay West looked nothing like a rugged cowboy and everything like a handsome prince. But she wasn't in the market for a prince. She didn't need anyone to ride to her rescue.

She'd been intrigued by the information that his mother had been an actress and it was part of that intrigue that had prompted the invitation for a drink with her.

For the first time since she'd met him, she realized she wanted to know more about him, more about his personal life and family. She told herself it was nothing more than idle curiosity, but suspected it was something more. She refused to dwell on what that something more might be.

"She's sound asleep," she said as she stepped into the room.

Clay whirled around from the window to face her, a smile curling his lips upward. God, it should be illegal for this man to smile, she thought as she headed toward the bar.

"She loved the movie," he said. "I think I even heard you laugh a time or two."

"You sound surprised." She moved toward the bar, conscious of his gaze following her. "I do laugh occasionally."

"Too occasionally," he replied, and joined her at the bar.

She poured herself a glass of wine. "What can I get for you? We're locked in for the night and the security system is on. Surely you can break down and have a cocktail with me."

He hesitated a moment, then nodded. "Okay. Scotch on the rocks." Again she was aware of his gaze lingering on her as she splashed the liquor into the bottom of a glass and added a couple of ice cubes.

Suddenly she thought maybe this idea of a little conversation and a drink was a bad one. Tonight there was something in his gaze that heated her blood, that made her feel just a little bit light-headed.

She handed him his drink and as their fingers brushed a jolt of electricity shot up her arm. She shouldn't be surprised. There had been a shimmering electricity in the air between them all evening.

She didn't begin to relax until she was seated in a chair and he on the sofa across from her. "Did you enjoy the evening?"

"It was all right," he replied, and tugged off the tie around his neck and unfastened the top two buttons of his shirt. "Although I'm always more comfortable when the attire isn't quite so formal." His gaze held hers for a long moment. "Red is definitely your color, Libby."

To her dismay, a blush warmed her cheeks. She couldn't remember the last time anyone had made her blush. "Thank you."

He settled back against the sofa, a picture of elegant but bold masculinity in his black tux against the white cushions. He took a deep drink from the glass of Scotch. "I'll tell you one thing, I've never seen a bigger bunch of dysfunctional people than the parents of the kids in Gracie's film."

An edge of defensiveness rose inside her. She took a sip of her wine before replying. "Why do you think they're dysfunctional? Because they want the best for their children? Because they're pursuing careers for their children that you don't approve of?"

He raised one dark eyebrow with a mocking smile.

"Are you telling me that you think Delores Gleason is well-adjusted?"

Despite her automatic defensiveness, a small laugh escaped her. "Okay, Delores might be the exception," she admitted. "Delores is the kind of stage mother who gives all of us a bad name. I'm nothing like Delores."

"No, you're much prettier." There was a teasing tone in his deep voice that she'd never heard before. Maybe the Scotch was going right to his head.

She certainly felt as if the wine had gone to hers. She felt too warm and tingly all over. "That's not the only difference between Delores and me," she replied. "Delores is dependent on her son financially. I don't depend on Gracie's money for anything."

"You mentioned something about investments?"

"I did two smart things when I first started making money here in Hollywood. I invested in a young designer's business and that designer now has clothing lines in all the major stores. The second thing I invested in was real estate."

"Smart woman," he said.

"Why don't you tell me about your family, Clay?" She didn't want to think about business tonight.

Clay had been in her home for almost a week and she really knew nothing about him other than his eyes often radiated an underlying sense of disapproval and something about him energized her in a way that wasn't unpleasant.

"What do you want to know about them?" he asked.

"You said your mother died when you were young. Did your father remarry?"

"No. Dad was a one-woman kind of man and he never even dated after my mother was gone."

"Must have been tough, being a single parent to so many kids."

He smiled and again she felt the power of that smile deep in the pit of her stomach. "He wasn't exactly a single parent. We had Smokey who barked at us kids like a drill sergeant."

"That would be the cranky cook Gracie has mentioned."

Clay nodded. "Smokey was a ranch manager years ago. A fall from his horse nearly killed him and when he recovered he moved into the house to become surrogate mother and cook for the family."

"What about your brothers and sister? Tell me about them." She liked the sound of his deep voice and wasn't ready to crawl into her cold, lonely bed yet.

"Tanner is the oldest. He's thirty-five and a typical first-born child, bossy as hell and controlling. Dalton is next. He's thirty-three and a copy of Tanner. Zack is thirty-one and full of fire."

The affection he felt for his siblings was obvious in the warmth of his voice as he spoke of them. A touch of envy swept through her. What might her life had been like if she'd had loving sisters or brothers to temper the cold disdain of her parents?

"Then there's Meredith," he continued. "She's twenty-seven and as the only girl she's both a tomboy and spoiled.

Finally there's Joshua, the baby of the family. He's twenty-five, spoiled rotten but a real charmer."

"And what about you? How would you characterize yourself?" She finished her wine and set the empty glass on a coaster on the nearby end table.

"Oh, I don't know. My family would say that I'm the one who always played well alone. I'm the quietest of the bunch. In fact, I was so quiet as a kid there were several times my father took us all to town and he'd be halfway home before he'd realize I wasn't in the car."

His words appalled her. "That's horrible," she exclaimed. She could well imagine how he must have felt because she'd always had the feeling when her parents took her to town they'd wished they could leave her somewhere where she'd never find her way back home.

"Not really," he replied. "I always knew my dad loved me and didn't mean to leave me behind."

There was a quiet confidence in his tone she envied, the confidence of a man who knew his place in life and was comfortable in his own skin. He'd probably never suffered a moment's doubt about who he was and where he was going. He'd probably never lain awake at night and worried about the decisions he'd made that day.

"What about you? What's your family like?" He finished his drink and placed his empty glass on the coaster on the coffee table.

She could tell it wasn't just a polite question, genuine curiosity shone from his green eyes. She couldn't remember the last time any man had been curious about anything coming out of her mouth other than business decisions concerning her daughter.

She thought about lying, thought about spinning some Hollywood fantasy of the perfect parents who had died tragically in some accident, parents she mourned to this very day. But Libby had never been one to lie, even in a town filled with liars.

"There's just me and my parents. They live in a small farming community in Pennsylvania."

"You aren't close?"

As always, thoughts of her parents created a knot of tension in the pit of her stomach. "Let's just say that from the moment I was born I proved to be a great disappointment to my parents. Our relationship right now is that once a month I send them a check and once a month they cash it."

She grabbed her glass from the end table and stood, irritated with herself for revealing as much as she had about a past she'd tried to forget.

She took her glass to the bar and he did the same, standing far too close to her at the sink. "Sounds like a childhood that wasn't much fun," he observed.

"I survived," she replied with a false lightness. "Besides, it's all in the past. I'm not that unhappy little girl anymore." Thinking about her past always made her feel cold and empty inside.

She stepped away from the sink, away from him. "And now I think it's time for me to say good-night. We have an early morning tomorrow with the photo shoot."

She was acutely aware of him, his scent, his nearness,

both invading her personal space in a way she rarely allowed as they left the living room.

When they reached the bottom of the stairs he took her arm, halting her progress toward her bedroom. There wasn't a trace of judgment in the depths of his deep green eyes, rather there was a hint of a compassion that reached inside to touch her heart.

"I'm sorry for you." His deep voice was just above a whisper and his fingers remained warm and inviting on her arm. "Every kid deserves a happy, carefree life full of un-conditional love."

He stepped even closer to her and she knew he was going to kiss her. More importantly she knew she was going to kiss him back.

Her heart quickened and her blood warmed as he placed a hand on her cheek and caressed the side of her face. "I might be the one my family says plays well alone, but I don't always like to play alone." With those words he pulled her into an embrace and took her mouth with his.

Even though she'd told herself differently, on some level she'd known that this kiss was inevitable. She'd tried to deny to herself the chemistry that had snapped in the air between them from the moment she had first seen him standing in her living room.

The kiss was affirmation of that chemistry. His lips plied hers with a heat that was intoxicating and she found herself leaning into him, wanting to get closer, wanting to be held tighter.

He must have felt the need in her and he complied,

tightening his arms and pulling her more firmly against his strong body.

As he deepened the kiss, his tongue tentatively touching hers, she could taste the Scotch he'd drunk. Still, she found the taste of his mouth provocative.

As she leaned into him she felt his arousal against her. She was turned on, as well. Her nipples pressed almost painfully taut against her wispy lace bra and she wanted his big strong hands touching her there…touching her everywhere.

He moaned, a small sound that heightened her desire as she wrapped her arms around his neck in an effort to pull him closer…closer still.

A crash resounded from upstairs, followed by the shattering of glass and the sharp blare of the house alarm. Above the din of the alarm Gracie's scream sliced the air. Libby gasped as Clay released her so abruptly she nearly fell.

Gracie! Libby's heart exploded with fear as Clay pulled a gun from an ankle holster and started up the stairs.

Chapter 6

Clay took the stairs two at a time while his finger flipped the safety off his revolver. His heartbeat crashed painfully hard in his chest as he ran toward Gracie's bedroom.

As he entered the room he flipped on the switch to turn on the ceiling light. "Mr. Clay!" Gracie cried from the bed.

Instant relief nearly buckled his knees as he saw that she appeared to be unharmed, but frightened. The cause of the crash and shattering glass was obvious. A large brick sat on the floor and the glass of the window in the bedroom lay in glittering shards on the carpet.

He heard Libby enter the room and glanced around to see her run to the bed to place an arm around Gracie. As she comforted the little girl, Clay walked through the broken glass toward the window where the balmy night air drifted inside.

He peered out, but the night darkness gave up no secrets. He saw nobody in the yard, nobody running from the house. He frowned, noting the distance from the street to this particular window. It would be impossible for that size brick to be thrown that distance. Somebody had gotten close…too close to the house.

The phone began to ring, the jangling barely audible with the din of the alarm resounding. "That will be the security company," Libby said. "There's a phone and a keypad in my bedroom."

"Stay here," he commanded, then hurried down the hallway toward her room.

The phone was on the nightstand next to the king-size bed. Clay answered, explained what had happened, then gave the code word that would let the security company know that no further action was necessary.

When he hung up the phone, he tucked his gun back into his ankle holster. He didn't know if Gracie had noticed it when he'd burst into her bedroom, but he didn't want her further frightened.

He saw the keypad Libby had indicated just inside the door of her room and punched in the numerical code that stopped the blare of the alarm. Blessed silence followed.

As he walked back toward the door of the bedroom, he couldn't help but notice the decor. Here, in the four walls of her bedroom was the evidence of a passionate woman.

A red-and-white satin spread covered the bed and the plump large pillows were in red satin pillowcases. Bright red floral arrangements and thick scented candles were scattered here and there, adding to the sensual look of the room.

It was easy to imagine her lying in the center of the big bed, clad in a silky nightgown with only the glow of the candles playing on her beautiful skin.

It was a slight shock; he'd expected her room to be impersonal, utilitarian. But what surprised him more was the passion he'd tasted in her lips only moments before. What shocked him even further was her lusty response to his kiss.

These thoughts flitted through his head as he hurried from her room and back to where Libby and Gracie awaited him. They were still on the bed, huddled together in the center with their arms wrapped around each other.

"Why don't the two of you go to your room for the rest of the night," he said to Libby. "I'm going to take a look outside. Lock yourself into your room."

"You'll let me know what you find?" she asked.

He nodded. "I'll let you know as soon as I get back into the house." He smiled at Gracie. "Looks like you're going to have a slumber party with your mom tonight."

"Okay, but why did somebody break my window?" Gracie asked.

"Come on, honey, we'll talk in my room," Libby said, apparently sensing Clay's desire to get outside as soon as possible.

She grabbed Gracie's favorite stuffed bunny then the two of them left the bed. Clay watched until they disappeared into Libby's bedroom, then he hurried down the stairs.

All thoughts of the kiss he'd shared with Libby disappeared as he went into the cold, determined mind-set of duty.

Protect and serve. It was the motto of policemen and armed forces, but it was also what Red West had instilled in his sons and daughter when it came to the business of being a bodyguard.

He once again pulled his gun as he stepped out the front door. He quietly closed and locked the door behind him. The warm night air whispered through the trees with just the softest of a breeze. The grounds were faintly illuminated with landscaping lights and he made his way silently across the manicured lawn.

He let his revolver lead the way even though he knew whoever had thrown the brick would be long gone by now. Still, he didn't intend to take any chances. There was no way anyone could get in through the tall security gates that guarded the driveway. Whoever had come on the property had to have come over the eight-foot wall that surrounded the place.

Standing in the grass, he stared up at Gracie's bedroom window. That brick had to have been thrown from the general area where Clay now stood and even then it would have taken a tremendous amount of effort…or rage.

He looked around in the grass, hoping to spot something, anything, that might have been accidentally dropped or fallen off the perpetrator.

What bothered him was that the brick had been thrown through Gracie's window. His bedroom window was on one side of hers and several other windows were also potential targets.

Was it just a coincidence that the brick had flown through Gracie's window or was it something more ominous? If Gracie's bed had been any closer to the window in the room, she might have been seriously hurt either by the brick itself or by the shattering glass.

Was this an isolated incident? Mischievous kids out to make trouble? If so, somebody had gone to a tremendous amount of trouble just to break a window…specifically Gracie's window.

He left the grounds by the driveway gate and walked the length of the wall, looking for some sign that somebody had gone over the top of it. But there was nothing.

Dammit, somebody had gotten too close.

There was nothing more he could do now but call the local authorities and make a report. He wanted an official record of anything that happened that was out of the ordinary.

Once he was back in the house, he checked the security system one last time to make certain it was armed, then went back upstairs.

He passed Gracie's bedroom and went down the hallway to Libby's door and knocked softly. She opened the door with her fingers to her lips, then slid out into the hall.

Gone was the drop-dead dress she'd worn to the premiere and in its place was a pink silk nightgown covered with a matching robe. The red dress had made her look vibrant and hot. The pink nightclothes made her look soft, feminine and oddly vulnerable.

"She's asleep," she said. "What did you find?"

"Nothing." He frowned and tried to keep his attention focused away from the slight gap in the robe that offered a glimpse of a barely covered full breast.

"Do you think this has something to do with the letters? You think maybe the same person who's been writing such hateful things did this?" A tiny wrinkle furrowed her brow as she gazed at him.

"I don't know. It's possible and then again this might just be some unrelated incident."

"Speaking of unrelated incidents, about what happened earlier." A blush reddened her cheeks.

"Are you talking about the kiss?" He raised an eyebrow. "Libby, don't tell me you're one of those women who enjoy a moment of honest emotion then spend the next week blaming it on too much wine or not enough sleep or any number of excuses that absolve you of any responsibility."

"Of course not." The pink of her cheeks deepened, but she met his gaze boldly. "I take fifty percent responsibility for that kiss. All I was going to say is that I'm not sure it's a good idea for us to explore whatever…whatever chemistry is at work between us."

"So you feel it, too." He was almost relieved to know that she felt the simmering tension that crackled in the air between them, that she was aware of the physical pull that existed.

"I'd have to be dead not to feel it," she said dryly. "But that doesn't mean it's smart to follow through on it."

"And you always do what's smart, right?"

"You make that sound like it's a bad thing," she replied.

"Not necessarily. I just think it sometimes doesn't hurt to let go of control, to go with the flow…"

"And sleep with you?"

He grinned. "You make that sound like it's a bad thing."

She laughed, that low, sexy laughter that spiked a renewed burst of desire through him. "I have a feeling there's a lot more to you than meets the eye."

"I have a feeling the same could be said for you." He took a step back from her and allowed his gaze to sweep her from head to toe. "All I know is that I figure we're both single, consenting adults, without any expectations of a future together. I want you, and if you feel the same about me then why not follow through on it?"

"All I intend to follow through on at the moment is getting a good night's sleep and I hope what you intend to follow though on is keeping my daughter safe."

How neatly she'd turned the conversation from personal matters to professional. "I'd do anything in my power to keep Gracie safe," he replied honestly. "And on that note, I need to call the local authorities and make a report of the broken window. Get some sleep and I'll see you in the morning."

"Good night, Clay." For just a brief moment he saw in her eyes a heat that made him want to grab her back into his arms and kiss her mindless.

But he didn't. The moment had passed, the mood had passed and it was time to shove want aside and get on with his job.

"Good night, Libby." He turned on his heels and went

The Bodyguard's Promise

into his bedroom where he used his cell phone to call the local police precinct. He made a report by phone, then changed from his tuxedo into a pair of jeans and a T-shirt.

He left his room and went back into Gracie's. He placed his gun on the nightstand and went back to the window, the broken glass crunching beneath his shoes.

Was it merely coincidence that it had been Gracie's window? Or was it something more sinister? Had the author of the letters escalated into a new kind of terror?

What concerned him most was that the letters that had been sent to Gracie had been mailed to her post office box. If the person who had smashed the window was the same person who was writing the letters, then that person now knew not only where Gracie lived but also which bedroom was hers.

At least they didn't have to worry about rain. The night was clear and cloudless. First thing in the morning he'd make sure a glass company was called to come and replace the window and a cleaning crew came in to deal with all the broken glass.

For now there was nothing more he could do except sleep in here and make certain nobody used the glassless window as an open invitation to come inside the house.

He moved away from the window and stretched out on Gracie's uncomfortably small bed. He found his thoughts returning to Libby and the kiss they had shared.

In a million years he never would have guessed that her lips would hold so much heat or that she'd press her body so intimately against his.

He certainly had no illusions about any real relationship developing between him and Libby. Although he usually didn't get involved with clients, he wouldn't mind a lusty physical encounter with the pretty blonde.

Her lifestyle did nothing for him, he didn't necessarily support the decisions she made for her daughter, but that didn't temper the fact that she turned him on as no other woman had in a very long time.

He'd told her that he was the kind of person who played well alone. He suspected she was the same kind of person. Neither of them was looking for anything permanent.

So what harm could come from making their Hollywood pretend affair real for the duration of his stay? He certainly wasn't worried about his heart getting involved with her and he suspected she didn't have much of a heart to get involved with him.

The man was getting under her skin. As if the devastating kiss hadn't been enough to unsettle her, he'd actually spoken out loud of his desire for her.

His words had kept her tossing and turning all night long as she'd tried to imagine what making love with him would be like. She now sat on the edge of her bed, lost in thoughts of a man who shouldn't be occupying her mind.

She had a feeling Clay West would be a masterful lover, one filled with a passion and energy that could make a woman lose her mind. There was something both frightening and inviting in the thought of losing herself in him.

Equally as frightening was that moment when she'd

heard the crash and the alarm had blared and Gracie's scream had sliced through her heart with a knife of sheer terror.

Whenever she thought of that brick on the floor, her blood chilled in her veins. What if it had hit Gracie in the head? What if the glass had cut her?

"Mommy!"

Libby blinked herself back to the here and now where Gracie was opening the box of clothing that had been sent by courier moments before from the Duggin's Dude Ranch people. The note that had accompanied the large box indicated that they hoped she would wear what was inside for the photo shoot that would be taking place in just a little over three hours from now.

"Look, there's a cool pair of jeans and a red-and-black blouse with fringe." Gracie pulled each item from the box with excitement. "And there's cowboy boots! Red cowboy boots," she squealed. "And a cowboy hat!"

She plopped the hat on her head. "I wanna show Mr. Clay. Maybe since I look like a real cowgirl he'll take us home with him and I can ride horses and feed cows and pull carrots out of Mr. Red's garden." Before Libby could respond, Gracie ran out of the bedroom in search of Clay.

Libby remained standing next to the bed, shocked by her daughter's words. It was the first time Gracie had ever expressed any kind of desire to be somewhere else, to do something other than make movies and commercials.

"Mommy, Mr. Clay has a cowboy hat, too!" Gracie called from the hallway.

Libby stepped outside of the bedroom to see Clay standing next to Gracie, a black cowboy hat pulled low on his brow. He looked bold and sexy and more than a little bit dangerous.

"If Mommy had a cowgirl hat, then we'd look like a family of cowboys," Gracie exclaimed.

"Gracie, honey. We've got to get moving," Libby said. "We've got the car coming in an hour and a half, and you still need to take a bath and get dressed."

"How's the work coming?" Libby asked Clay as Gracie ran back down the hallway toward her mother's bedroom.

He took the hat off his head. "They're just about finished installing the new window then the cleanup crew can finish up their work. They should be done by the time we have to leave."

"Good, I wouldn't be comfortable leaving the house with strangers working here while we're gone."

"That isn't going to happen," he assured her. "When we leave, everyone leaves."

She flashed him a quick smile. "I've got to get Gracie into the tub."

"Go on. I'll just get back to supervising the work in Gracie's bedroom."

As Libby hurried back to her bedroom to help Gracie get ready for her work that day, she was pleased that the morning had brought no discomfort between herself and Clay. Breakfast had been pleasant, with easy conversation and no overt reference to the kiss and conversation they'd shared the night before.

She refused to be the kind of woman he'd talked about last night, the kind of woman who gave in to passion, then whined about the consequences. If and when she decided to sleep with Clay, there would be no morning regrets. She never made decisions she regretted.

The morning passed quickly as she worked to get Gracie ready for the photo shoot. At some point she was aware of the doorbell ringing, but she ignored it. Clay had made it clear from the very beginning of his stay here that he would be in charge of answering the door.

"Mommy, you have to wear jeans, too," Gracie said. She sat on the edge of Libby's bed, looking far too pretty to be a cowgirl. Her long blond hair fell in springy curls over her shoulders and her eyes held the excitement of the job ahead.

Libby, on the other hand, had scarcely had time to even look at herself in the mirror. She stood in front of her closet clad in bra and panties, trying to decide what to put on.

"Jeans, huh?"

"Yes, I'm wearing jeans and Mr. Clay is wearing jeans, so it would be good if you did, too," Gracie said. "Then we'd all look alike."

Why not? Libby thought. It wasn't as though anyone was going to be taking her picture, and the photo shoot was for a dude ranch. "All right, jeans it is," she agreed.

It took her several minutes of digging in the closet to find a pair of jeans and a red-and-white-striped casual blouse to go with them. Aware that the car would be arriving at any moment she flew into the bathroom and dabbed on minimal makeup, then pulled her long hair into a clip at the nape of her neck.

The phone rang and she answered. The car had arrived. "Come on, sweetheart, our chariot has arrived," she said to her daughter.

As they exited the bedroom, Libby was struck with an unexpected cold rush of fear. Was this photo shoot a mistake? The Hollywood Walk of Fame was about as public a place as there could be. Was she putting Gracie at risk by allowing this to take place?

She thought perhaps the incident from the night before had affected her more than she'd realized. As much as she tried to tell herself it had nothing to do with the threatening letters, she couldn't quite convince herself of that fact.

Clay met them in the hallway and just the sight of him, so big and strong, so confident and capable, eased some of the fear inside her.

He carried with him a large box and as they approached where he stood, he held it out to her. "What's this?" She frowned in confusion as she took the box from him.

"Something I had delivered a little while ago."

"Open it, Mommy!" Gracie clapped her hands together with excitement.

Libby set the box on the floor and opened the flaps to reveal a red Stetson cowboy hat. Her heart fluttered with as much feminine pleasure as if the box contained exotic cut flowers or a diamond necklace.

"It's a hat like mine," Gracie exclaimed.

"Indeed, it is," Libby replied as she pulled the hat from its tissue-lined container. "Thank you, Clay. That was very thoughtful." She placed the hat on her head.

He shrugged. "I figured we all might as well look like a bunch of wranglers straight off the ranch and now we'd better get downstairs. The car is waiting."

As Libby walked down the stairs she realized that if she wasn't careful this man could have the potential to do what no man had done in a very long time. If she wasn't careful, Clay West might walk right into her heart.

Although Clay wasn't thrilled with the open area where the photo shoot was to take place, he was at least pleased to see a handful of police officers on site, keeping the gathering crowd of onlookers behind velvet-covered ropes tied to movable poles.

As they exited the car in front of where the shoot was to take place, the crowd began to yell Gracie's name. Libby whisked her daughter ahead of her as he walked behind and scanned the area for any potential trouble.

The photographer awaited, as did the horse upon which Gracie would sit to have her photo taken. The horse was tall and noble-looking but with a sway back that identified it as an old nag accustomed to carrying riders of all sizes and shapes.

The people gathering to watch the action appeared to be mostly tourists with cameras slung around their necks and flowered shirts that screamed sightseers.

There had been no publicity concerning the photo

shoot, no way anyone would know ahead of time that Gracie was going to be here unless Libby had told somebody, and Libby wasn't given to sharing information with anyone.

That, at least, gave Clay some small measure of relief. He walked over to where Libby and Gracie stood, Libby talking to the photographer.

With the tight jeans encasing her long legs and emphasizing her tight shapely butt, with her full breasts pressed against the cotton material of her blouse and that cowboy hat riding her head, she was the epitome of every cowboy's wet dream.

A tug on his belt called his attention to Gracie, who looked up at him with a worried gaze. "Mr. Clay? Would you pick me up? I need to whisper in your ear."

Clay hefted her into his arms and onto one hip. She clung to him like a little monkey. "What's wrong, honey?" he asked.

She cupped her hands and placed her mouth against his ear. "I'm scared," she whispered.

He leaned his head back and looked at her in surprise. "You're scared? Of what?"

She pointed a finger in the direction of the horse. "It's so big."

He felt the tremble in her body and he realized how big that horse would look to a little girl who had never been around a horse in her life.

"Honey, that horse might be big, but I can tell by looking in her eyes that she's really sweet." Gracie looked at him skeptically and he continued. "You know I'm a real rootin' tootin' cowboy and I know horses. I can tell just by looking at a horse if she's nice or if she's mean." He pointed to the horse in question. "And that's one sweet lady."

"Really?" Gracie looked at him hopefully.

"How about I take you over there and we get acquainted with the horse before you need to sit on her."

"Okay." Gracie tightened her grip around his neck as he carried her to where the horse and a young man stood awaiting their jobs for the day.

"Hi," the young man said, a friendly smile lighting his face. "I'm Stony, one of the ranch hands for Duggin's Dude Ranches."

"Hi, I'm Clay and this is…"

"Gracie, yeah I know." He smiled at Gracie. "I've seen a couple of your movies."

"And what's this girl's name?" Clay stroked the horse's brow as Gracie watched with widened eyes.

"Sugar," Stony replied. "Because she's sweet as candy."

"Hear that, Gracie? I told you she looked like a sweet lady. You want to pet her?" Clay asked.

Gracie hesitantly held out a hand then rubbed it over the horse's forehead. The horse whinnied softly and Gracie giggled. "She's talking."

"She's telling you that it's nice to meet you and she likes you," Clay said. He felt the tense little muscles in her body relax.

"I love horses," she said.

Clay laughed, finding Gracie delightful as always.

At that moment the photographer and Libby came to where he and Gracie stood and the preparations for the photo shoot began.

As a makeup lady attended to Gracie's face and a photographer's assistant measured the light source, Libby stood next to Clay and looked up at him.

"For somebody who told me you didn't work with kids, you're very good with them," she said.

He grinned at her. "It's easy with Gracie. Sometimes I get the feeling she isn't a kid but rather a miniature grown-up."

"You haven't seen one of her childish temper tantrums yet," Libby said dryly.

He smiled, his gaze on Gracie who now sat on the back of Sugar. "She's a sweet kid." She was a sweet kid thrust into a cutthroat world and he found himself wondering how she'd fare in the future.

The photo shoot took over an hour and Clay was surprised at Gracie's professionalism. Not once did she whine or complain as the photographer manipulated her into different positions, telling her to lift her head, drop her chin, move a shoulder and smile. And she did smile, the beatific smile of somebody doing what they loved.

"Libby, Clay…come on over and I'll do a group shot of the three of you," the photographer said after announcing he'd gotten some great shots for the ad.

"Come on Mommy and Mr. Clay," Gracie exclaimed. "Come get your picture taken with me."

"You go on," he said to Libby. "It would make a nice shot of mother and daughter cowgirls."

"Mr. Clay, I want you, too!" Gracie said.

"You don't need me in the picture," Clay protested.

"But I want a picture of the three of us and I'll frame it and put it next to my bed." Her lips turned downward and the lower one began to quiver. "Please, Mr. Clay. I want a picture of you."

He laughed and shook a finger at her. "Save those pretend tears, little girl, they don't work with me."

Gracie grinned like a kid caught with her hand in the cookie jar. "I won't pretend cry if you come and get in the picture with me and Mommy."

Relenting, Clay started forward but as he took his first step a sharp report rang out. With a burst of frantic adrenaline, he dived for Gracie.

Chapter 7

Everything seemed to go in slow motion for Libby. People screamed and ducked and she watched helplessly as Clay went headfirst over the back of the horse to grab Gracie. Together they tumbled to the sidewalk on the other side of the horse, Gracie sheltered in his arms as he took the brunt of the fall.

Libby was yanked down, by whom she wasn't sure. She didn't stay down. She needed to get to Gracie.

The security guards went into action, moving people further back from the area as police officers began to comb through the crowd.

Had it been a shot? Had somebody fired a gun? Her heart thudded wildly as she got up and ran around the skittish horse where Clay was getting up, his features set in stone.

Gracie was crying, although it was obvious she wasn't hurt but merely frightened. She clung to Clay, her little arms tight around his neck as he got to his feet.

"We need to get her out of here," Clay said as Libby reached him.

She nodded and held out her arms to take Gracie. "I've got her," he said. "Let's go."

As they headed for the awaiting car, he kept the child against him, his big arms wrapped around her back as if to shield her from any danger that might still come.

Libby hurried just behind them, her heart racing so fast she felt physically ill. Surely it had been nothing more than the backfire of a car or something else equally benign. But it hadn't sounded like a car backfire. It had sounded like a gunshot.

Clay got into the car with Gracie and Libby followed, not breathing easily until the driver pulled into the street and away from the scene with a screech of tires.

"Why did you do that, Mr. Clay?" Gracie exclaimed as she sat up on his lap. "These are real tears, not pretend. You scared me."

"I'm sorry, honey. I didn't mean to scare you," he said, his stony countenance softening as he looked at Gracie. "But I needed to get you off that horse really fast."

"You could have just told me to get down," she said with an indignant sniff. She crawled off Clay's lap and moved to sit next to Libby.

Libby wrapped an arm around her daughter, consciously not squeezing too tight although she wanted to wrap Gracie up in her arms and never let her go. She needed to smell the familiar scent of her child and to assure herself that Gracie was truly all right.

"Mr. Clay didn't have time to tell you to get off," she said. "And he certainly didn't scare you on purpose."

"I didn't even get to tell Sugar goodbye," Gracie said.

"Sugar knew we had to leave in a hurry," Clay replied.

Libby shot him a grateful smile, a smile that transformed to a gasp as she saw his bloody elbows and forearms. "Oh, Clay, you're hurt." She dug in her purse for tissues and handed them to him.

"Just torn up a bit. It's mostly superficial." He dabbed the wounds with the tissue.

Gracie scooted across the seat to his side. "Oh, Mr. Clay," she said mournfully with huge eyes. "You've got bad boo-boos."

He smiled. "It's all right. Cowboys are tough."

"Won't the police want to talk to us?" Libby asked. "We ran out of there so fast." Her mind still worked to make sense of what had just happened.

Had somebody taken a shot at her baby? Had the person who had been writing those letters finally gone off the deep end? The thought terrified her. If it hadn't been for Clay's quick reaction, would Gracie now be on her way to an emergency room?

"I'm sure if it's necessary somebody will contact us."

They didn't speak any more of the incident for the rest of the ride home. Libby was grateful that Gracie seemed to have no idea what had just transpired. She wasn't sure how you explained to an eight-year-old little girl that somebody wanted to harm her.

When they got into the house, Molly, the young woman who acted as maid, nanny and all-around helper, appeared at the door to greet them.

"Molly, why don't you take Gracie upstairs to her room? See that she changes into play clothes and play a game or two with her," Libby instructed.

"Come on, Molly, we can play dolls because Mr. Clay won't play that with me." Gracie caught Molly's hand in hers and the two started up the stairs.

Libby turned to Clay. "And you, come with me." He crooked a dark eyebrow upward, but didn't speak as he followed her up the stairs and into her bedroom.

"I've always enjoyed matinees," he finally said, a definite twinkle in his eyes.

She scowled at him and tried to ignore the flash of heat his words inspired. "This is strictly a medical emergency." She pointed him toward the adjoining bathroom.

She indicated that he sit on the edge of the tub while she bent beneath the sink counter to get out peroxide, anti-biotic cream and cotton balls.

"I figure if you're hurt in the line of duty the least I can do is clean your wounds," she said.

He held out his bloody elbows. "You aren't the type to faint at the sight of blood?"

She uncapped the peroxide bottle, soaked a cotton ball and began to clean one of his elbows. "Not hardly. I was raised on a farm where every Sunday my mother butchered a chicken. You can't grow up on a working farm and have a weak stomach."

At the moment she had no visceral response to the sight of his torn-up elbow, but the warmth of his body so close to her, the scent of his cologne and the slightly wicked glint in his eyes all combined to make her feel half breathless and off center.

"Do you miss it? Life on the farm?" he asked.

The question instantly threw her back in time and, as always when she thought of her childhood, an overwhelming loneliness filled her soul.

Memories of working in the garden, the sun hot on her back flashed through her mind. She hadn't minded the work, but she'd longed for her mother to talk to her, to look at her.

Silent meals, silent evenings with her father reading the paper and her mother sewing or quilting, their foreheads ridged with permanent frown lines.

There were no memories of warm moments between her parents and her, no happy remembrances of a childhood long gone, only silence, censure and loneliness.

"No, I don't miss it. Do you think it was a gunshot?" she asked, needing to focus on anything but him or her past. She finished cleaning one elbow and began on the other.

He remained silent for a long moment, his gaze intent on her face as if he were seeking answers to some unspoken question.

"I don't know," he finally replied. "I thought so at the

time, but it all happened so fast and I wasn't taking any chances." He gazed at her soberly and she noticed that his eyes weren't just plain green, but rather held splashes of gold flecks. "Who knew about the photo shoot?"

She finished with the peroxide, then opened the tube of antibiotic cream. "Charlie, of course. He's the one who set it up. I might have mentioned it to Jordan. He'd want to know anything the kids were involved in while the movie was being shot."

She dabbed on the cream, frowning thoughtfully as she tried to remember who might have known about the photo shoot. "I don't know who else might have known," she said as she finished dabbing the cream on his wounds.

She screwed on the lid and stepped back from him, finding it easier to breathe, easier to think with some distance. "I don't know who Charlie or Jordan might have told, nor do I know who the people from Duggin's Dude Ranch might have mentioned it to."

"What about your driver? Was he on the list of people you gave me?"

"Raymond? Yes, I'm sure he was. He has impeccable references and I can't imagine him having any reason to want to harm Gracie."

He stood, but anything he might have said was halted by the ring of the telephone. It was the line that indicated somebody was at the front gates. Libby answered. It was a police officer. She buzzed him through, then turned back to Clay.

"It's one of Hollywood's finest," she said.

He nodded, obviously not surprised by a follow-up visit from a cop after the events that had just occurred. "Maybe we'll know after talking to him if it was a gunshot or not."

As they left the bedroom they met Molly and Gracie in the hallway. Both were clad in bathing suits and clutching towels. "Gracie wanted to swim," Molly said. "We were just coming to find you to see if it was okay."

"It's fine," Libby replied. She bent and kissed her daughter on the cheek. "Maybe when I get finished with some business I'll come out and swim with you."

Gracie smiled. "That would be so fun," she exclaimed. "And Mr. Clay, too."

"Oh, I don't know about that," Clay said.

"Please, Mr. Clay." Gracie grabbed one of his hands and gazed up at him with longing. "If you can't swim, I could teach you how. Mommy says I swim like a fish."

Libby watched Clay gaze at her daughter, a softness to his features that was there only when he interacted with the little girl. "You might be able to talk me into a dip in the pool," he relented.

"Hurray!" Gracie exclaimed.

"You and Molly go on out and we'll be out later," Libby said. As the two ran down the stairs, she smiled at Clay. "I think my daughter has managed to twist you around her little finger."

Again that soft look drifted into his eyes and his lips curved into a smile. "I never knew it could be like this with a kid. I never imagined how easily a little girl could work her way into my heart, how easily a little girl would find it to like a big lug like me."

"Children and puppies, they both have the same amazing ability to love unconditionally. There's nothing as pure or as wonderful in the world," Libby replied as they walked down the stairs.

Clay West without a shirt was amazing, Clay in a tuxedo was breath-taking, but Clay West talking about how much he cared for her daughter nearly stole her breath away.

Gracie had never seemed to notice the absence of a daddy in her life. She'd asked about her father only once and had seemed satisfied when Libby had told her that he lived very far away.

But she'd seen how Gracie gravitated toward Clay with a touch of hunger. She'd watched Gracie getting closer and closer to Clay and worried about how Gracie would handle Clay eventually leaving them to return to his life in Cotter Creek, Oklahoma.

And he would leave. She couldn't forget the fact that he was here to do a job and when the job was over he'd be gone. While that made him a certain liability where Gracie was concerned, it also made him perfect for a brief affair for Libby.

She wasn't looking for a happily-ever-after with a man. She'd decided a long time ago to devote herself to Gracie's happiness, to Gracie's future. There wasn't time to sustain any kind of a long-term relationship with any man.

And that made Clay West perfect for her.

She realized as she entered the living room and Clay

went to answer the door that it was far easier to think about Clay than to dwell on what had happened at the end of the photo shoot.

As she thought of those moments of terror when she'd watched Clay grab Gracie off the horse and shield her with his body, her heart once again began the frantic beat of uncertainty.

Had the policeman arrived to tell them that it had, indeed, been a gunshot, that the bullet had come within inches of hitting Gracie?

One thing was clear, had she had any doubts at all about Clay's commitment to Gracie's safety, they had been answered in a single instant that afternoon. Without thought for his own personal safety, Clay had thrown himself at Gracie, shielding her from potential harm.

She extended a hand to the officer who followed Clay into the living room. Officer Benjamin Walters introduced himself to both Clay and her.

"I'm here just to check to make sure you're all right," he said. "Unfortunately, there was a gentleman in the crowd promoting a new shoot 'em up independent Western film and he had a gun that fired blanks."

"That's damned irresponsible in a crowd of people," Clay said as relief coursed through Libby.

"It also got him arrested for disturbing the peace, among other charges." Officer Walters offered them a tight smile. "We just wanted to make certain that little Gracie and you were assured that we've taken care of the situation."

"Thank you, Officer Walters, I appreciate you stopping by," Libby replied.

"I'll walk you out," Clay said, and the two men left the living room and headed back toward the front door.

Libby turned to look out the windows, where she could see Gracie and Molly in the pool. Both were floating on rafts, but it was her daughter who held her attention.

She smiled as Gracie laughed and splashed Molly. Gracie had been the only person in her life who had taught Libby to love and the love she had in her heart for Gracie was so intense it was almost frightening.

She might have allowed Clay into her life for a brief period of time and she might invite him to her bed for an equally short time. But she knew in the end it would be as it had been for the past eight years of her life…she and Gracie against the world.

The swimming had been a bad idea, Clay thought as he sat on a deck chair and watched Libby and Gracie in the pool. He'd thought Libby looked hot in the turquoise bikini she'd worn when he'd first met her, but now wearing a hot-pink, two-piece suit, her lush near-naked curves were more eye candy than he'd enjoyed in a very long time.

Unfortunately the result of the view became not only painfully uncomfortable but also potentially embarrassing, as well. It didn't help matters that it had been far too long since he'd been with a woman. Still, he had a feeling even if he'd had a woman the night before, Libby Bryant would stir him all over again.

It didn't take long before he dived in, hoping the cold pool water would have a desirable result. Thankfully, it did.

As Gracie and Libby played in the shallow end of the pool, Clay did several laps, expending pent-up energy that had built to massive proportions.

The energy had begun the moment he'd heard the sound of that gun, then a new kind of energy had appeared as he'd sat while Libby tended to his wounds.

Just looking at her created a ball of tension in the pit of his stomach, smelling her scent increased that tension to painful heights.

As she'd cleaned his elbows he'd watched a pulse tick in the hollow of her throat, had felt the slight tremble of her fingers against his skin. He had a feeling she wanted him as badly as he wanted her, but as far as he was concerned the next step was up to her.

"Let's play Marco Polo," Gracie said when he'd finished his laps. "Come on, Mr. Clay, close your eyes and try to find us."

Dutifully, Clay closed his eyes. "Marco," he said.

"Polo." The responding answer came from either side of the pool. Gracie was on his left and Libby was on his right. He dived to the left, chasing Gracie with his eyes still closed. He didn't have to bother calling out "Marco" again. He could easily find the little girl by her excited giggling.

Once he'd caught Gracie, he went after Libby. She was slyer, not making a sound until he called out Marco and she was forced by the game rules to reply.

When he caught her, he circled his arms around her, his hands on her slick, wet back as her hands rested on his chest. "Gotcha," he murmured as Gracie squealed in delight from nearby.

"I guess you do," she replied, her voice slightly husky. Without warning, she dived down, out of his arms, and re-surfaced on the other side of the pool.

Despite the cold water that surrounded him, Clay was hard as a rock, wanting with an intensity he'd never felt before.

"Now it's my turn to be Marco," Gracie said.

They played in the water for another hour, then Libby and Clay got out and sat on the lounge chairs while Gracie paddled around the shallow end of the pool.

For the first time since he'd come to the house, they talked of nothing important. They talked about the weather and about favorite foods. They shared thoughts about old movies, new books and just life in general.

Dinner was served at one of the umbrella tables that dotted the pool area. By the time they finished eating, the sun was setting and Gracie was drooping with exhaustion.

As Libby and Gracie went upstairs to shower and get Gracie ready for bed, Clay walked around the house, checking to make certain the doors were locked.

At least he didn't have to worry too much about anyone getting into the house. The doors and windows had heavy-duty locks and the security system was state-of-the-art.

When he was certain that everything was secure, he went up to his room to shower off the chlorine from the pool. He stood beneath the hot spray and tried to keep his thoughts away from Libby.

He had almost decided that he'd been wrong in his assessment of the level of the threat in the letters that Gracie had received. He'd almost convinced himself that he'd overreacted, that the escalating rage had been nothing more than a figment of his imagination. Then that brick had sailed through the window.

Although the possibility existed that the brick had nothing to do with the letters, Clay's gut instinct told him otherwise. Somebody didn't like Gracie and he had a feeling the brick had only been the first display of dark emotions raging out of control.

The problem was, he didn't know how to protect Gracie. He didn't know who to protect her from. She was surrounded by people who may or may not have her best interests at heart. For many of those people she was nothing but a product, a hot commodity to be bought and sold to the highest bidder.

Even Libby, who he had no doubt loved her daughter, had a vested interest in the decisions she made for Gracie. Even though she'd protested that she wasn't a stage mother, he found it difficult to think of her as anything but that.

He respected her intelligence, enjoyed her wit, lusted for her on a physical level, but wasn't sure he respected the choices she made for her daughter when it came to this Hollywood lifestyle. He shut off the shower and grabbed a towel.

He was tired. It had been an unusually long day and between the adrenaline he'd expended when he'd heard that gunshot and the swimming, exhaustion weighed heavily on his shoulders.

Part of the exhaustion was mental. There was an edge of anticipation inside him, a need to know what might happen next. Although he was grateful that the shot this morning had been nothing but a stupid publicity stunt, he hadn't lost sight of the fact that he believed somebody posed a real threat to Gracie. The problem was finding who that somebody was and stopping them before anything happened.

Gracie. His heart softened at thoughts of her. Who would have thought that an eight-year-old would entrench herself so firmly into his heart?

He'd never dreamed a relationship with a kid could be so terrific. He'd never imagined that a smile from a little girl could somehow, at least momentarily, make things right with the world.

It would be hard to tell her goodbye, but Clay was accustomed to bidding clients farewell. His work as a bodyguard always culminated in a parting of the ways, but he had a feeling this one would be more difficult than the rest.

He'd just pulled on jeans and a T-shirt when a soft knock fell on his door. He opened the door to see Libby on the other side. She'd showered and changed into a long, sleeveless, light blue dress that electrified the color of her eyes and hugged each and every curve of her body. His exhaustion instantly slid away.

"She wants you to tell her good-night," she said.

"This is beginning to feel like a habit," he replied, and tried to keep his gaze off the thrust of her breasts against the cotton material.

She must have seen the surreptitious slide of his gaze because a faint pink stained her cheeks. "I think she likes to hear your stories of the ranch before she goes to sleep."

"Personally, I think I bore her to sleep," he said as they left his room and headed into one of the spare rooms where Gracie slept since the brick had flown through her bedroom window.

Gracie greeted him with a sleepy smile and as he settled into the chair next to the bed, Libby stood nearby, a definite distraction.

He started talking, telling Gracie more about his life at home. He told her stories about Smokey, the cranky cook with the heart of gold, then he told her about his brother Tanner working for a princess from a faraway country, who eventually became his bride.

As he spoke he tried to keep his attention off Libby, but it was an impossible task. Her very presence called to him; there appeared to be a smoldering in her eyes he'd never noticed before.

He was almost grateful when Gracie fell asleep and he could seek an escape. Libby followed him out into the hallway and as he started toward his bedroom she softly called his name. He turned to look at her, every muscle in his body painfully tense.

She licked her lower lip, a gesture he read as more nervous than seductive. "Now that you've tucked my daughter into bed I was wondering if you'd be interested in tucking me in?"

Chapter 8

Libby held her breath as she waited for his response. She didn't have to wait long. His eyes flared hot and wide and in two determined strides he was mere inches in front of her.

"Trust me when I tell you I won't tuck you in with a bedtime story and a kiss on the forehead," he said, his voice low and husky.

"Thank goodness," she responded. The words barely left her before he wrapped her up in his arms and took her mouth with his.

If she'd had any doubt as to what she was doing, those doubts were smothered by the raw hunger in his kiss, the sweep of his fevered hands down the length of her back.

It was rare that Libby did anything for herself. In every

move she'd made in the past eight years, in every decision she'd made, she'd always had Gracie's interests at heart.

But this was strictly for her and had nothing to do with Gracie. This was nothing but selfish need that she'd decided to indulge. She'd been on a slow simmer since the moment she'd laid eyes on him. Now, beneath the heat of his kiss, that simmer exploded into a full boil.

He tore his mouth from hers long before she was ready for him to and, without taking a breath, picked her up in his arms. Never in her life had any man swooped her up and carried her anywhere.

The walk down the hallway to her bedroom seemed interminably long and her heart raced knowing what would happen when he reached her room, her bed.

Once they got to her room he set her down on the floor next to the bed and once again captured her lips with a kiss that seared her down to her toes.

His tongue danced with hers as his hands went from the center of her back down to rest on the top of her hips. He pulled her closer, close enough that she could feel that he was aroused.

The feel of him, so hard against her, shot her own desire higher, hotter. She leaned into him, allowing herself to be swept away by the moment, by the man.

There would be no recriminations later. She wanted this. She'd wanted him since the moment she'd walked out of her office and had seen him standing in front of her so handsome, so strong.

She knew exactly what she was doing and she consciously gave up control to him, trusting that he understood that this was a single moment in time with no promise for anything more.

As the kiss continued, his hands moved down to cup her buttocks and he pulled her against him as his breathing became ragged and uneven.

He finally tore his mouth from hers and stared at her, his hunger in the depths of his green eyes. "I've wanted you since the first moment I saw you," he said.

His deep, sexy voice, coupled with the look in his eyes, sent shivers racing up her spine. "I've never wanted anyone as much as I do you right now," she confessed, her own voice breathless and throaty.

He dropped his hands and took a step back from her. With his gaze still locked with hers he pulled his T-shirt over his head. In the pale golden glow of the bedside lamp he looked nothing short of magnificent.

She feasted on the sight of his bare chest, broad and muscled with just a touch of springy dark hair in the center. Her fingers itched to coil themselves in the hair, to feel his heartbeat banging rapidly against her fingertips.

His hands moved to the snap of his jeans, but she stepped forward and shoved his hands away. She didn't intend to be a passive partner, but rather an active one, and she wanted to be the one to unfasten his jeans.

As her fingers touched the snap, he sucked in his breath, every muscle in his body stiff. Her fingers trembled as she unfastened the button, then unzipped his fly. When his jeans were hanging open, she ran her hands upward.

His skin felt fevered and the heat radiated into her, centering into a ball of fire at the very core of her. He captured her wrists and released a deep, ragged breath.

With a quick motion he spun her around so that her back was to him. Slowly, torturously, he unzipped her dress and as each inch of skin was revealed she felt the hot press of his lips against it.

Her knees weakened at the exquisite sensual pleasure as his mouth nipped and kissed the length of her back. When the zipper was all the way down, he turned her to face him, then pulled the dress from her shoulders.

It slid down her body and pooled at her feet, leaving her clad only in a light blue, wispy lace bra and matching bikini panties. Her taut nipples pressed against the bra and as his gaze lingered there, they became impossibly, almost painfully hard.

For a brief moment neither of them moved, then he groaned and that snapped the momentary inertia that had struck them. He kicked off his shoes and tore off his jeans as she yanked down the bedspread. He put his wallet on the nightstand, then together they tumbled into the bed, arms and legs entwined and lips locked in a kiss that ripped the last of rational thought from her mind.

She had wondered what kind of a lover he'd prove to be and it didn't take her long to have her answer. There was nothing fast or frantic about his caresses, rather they were slow and languid in an effort to evoke as much pleasure as possible.

It didn't take long for him to remove her bra and replace

the material with the heat of his mouth. Her breasts had never been so sensitive and she cried out with pleasure as his tongue paid particular attention to the pebble-hard nipples.

He slid his hands down her stomach where his fingers toyed along the band of her panties. He teased the skin just above the band until she thought she might go mad.

She returned the favor, raking her fingertips just above the band of his boxers, loving the sound of his deep moans as she finally touched him through the material.

"You're killing me," he whispered as she stroked the length of him.

"Then do something about it." The words were barely out of her mouth before he yanked off the boxers, then pulled off her bikinis.

He grabbed his wallet and opened it to withdraw a foil condom packet. She breathed a sigh of relief. She hadn't even thought about protection but was grateful he was thinking clearly for both of them.

She took the packet from him and ripped it open, then rolled the condom on him. By the time she was finished she could feel the imminent disintegration of his control.

His eyes flared as he positioned himself on top of her and, with the sigh of a man finally home, he entered her. For a long, breathtaking moment neither of them moved.

Libby closed her eyes and memorized every sweet sensation, the pounding of his heart against hers, the scent of him that filled the air and the warmth of his body against hers, in hers.

Then he moved and consciousness fell away as an explosion of pleasure swept over her, through her. His strokes were slow and controlled, creating a growing fervor in her.

She met his hips with thrusts of her own, increasing the pace as her need grew. She had passed the point of wanting slow and sweet. She wanted hot, fast and furious.

He must have sensed her need, for he moved faster, deeper, until she was crying out his name as the waves of release drowned her. At the same time she was conscious of him stiffening against her, then with a deep shudder he half collapsed onto her.

"I knew it would be good with you," he said when he'd managed to catch his breath. He raised up enough so he could see her face. "It was good, wasn't it?"

"It was better than good."

He nodded, as if satisfied, then got up and padded into her bathroom. As he closed the door behind him she wondered if he'd now go to his own room, his own bed. If he did, she was okay with that. She'd wanted sex with him, but she wasn't particularly interested in intimacy.

He came out of the bathroom, but instead of reaching for his clothes to dress, he turned off the lamp, then slid back beneath the sheets and gathered her into his arms.

She stiffened slightly, then relaxed into him as he began to stroke her hair. Okay, so a little bit of intimacy didn't hurt, she thought.

"Do you always carry condoms in your wallet?" she asked.

"Always. It was one of my father's and Smokey's

cardinal rules, that each of us boys always have no less than five condoms in our wallet whenever we left the house."

"Five? You all must have had a reputation for being quite the studs," she teased.

"You make that sound like a bad thing." He laughed and she loved the feel of the laughter deep in his chest. "I think my father and Smokey were just trying to keep us from having children before we were ready to have children."

"So, you have four more condoms in your wallet?"

His arms tightened around her. "That's right. Why, you got something in mind?"

It was her turn to laugh. "Not right now. I'm exhausted."

He held her for a long moment in silence. "What made you decide to be an actress?" he asked. "I mean, how did you get from a little farm in Pennsylvania to Hollywood?"

She ran her fingers through his tuft of chest hair and raised up just a bit to look at him. "Have you ever had a passion, Clay? Have you ever felt passionate about anything? Have you ever wanted to do something as much as you wanted to breathe?"

He regarded her soberly, then shook his head. "Honestly, no. I don't think I've ever felt passionately about anything."

"Then you probably won't understand," she said with a frown. "But I think I was born with a passion for acting. I was fascinated by television and would mimic lines and facial expressions. When I got older I wanted to try out for the local theater, but my parents refused to let me."

She rolled away from him. As always, when thinking of her childhood, a vast, dark loneliness filled her soul. "They forbid me to join in school plays, go to the movies or have anything to do with my dream."

She sighed. "They weren't really bad people, they were just life-weary and without dreams, and constantly told me there was nothing special about me, that the dreams I had were foolish ones." She looked at Clay once again. "Just because they forbid me to have anything to do with movies and theater didn't mean I stopped wanting." She smiled. "Whenever we went into town I'd sneak a couple of tabloids from the grocery store and stick them under my shirt."

"So I'm sleeping with a shoplifter," he said.

"It's not something I'm proud of and once I started earning some money I sent Mr. Willowby, the owner of the store, a check to cover every magazine I'd ever taken."

He pulled her back into his arms and she snuggled against his side as she continued talking. "I'd spend hours up in the hayloft poring over those tabloids, reading movie news and gossip. No matter what my parents told me, I knew I was going to be an actress. When Gracie was still a baby, I left home and came here."

"Big step for a single parent from a small town," he observed.

"I was terrified," she admitted. "I didn't know a soul and I didn't have just myself to think about, but also a baby.

And I was incredibly lucky. Almost immediately I found work and every dime I made that we didn't need to live on I invested. Apparently I have a knack for investments. I made a ton of money."

"But you quit acting."

As he continued to stroke her hair she found herself getting more and more sleepy, but she fought against it. She'd never talked about these things to anyone. She'd never been so open with anyone, but she trusted Clay on a level she'd never trusted before.

"When Gracie was two, I had a commercial shoot and had to take Gracie with me. The producer saw her and instantly wanted to hire her for a series of baby food commercials. Gracie was a natural, a born ham, and talented. She loved it and I saw in her the same passion I'd felt. I realized my parents had been right. I wasn't anything special, but Gracie was, so I decided to devote myself to her passion."

"And you're happy with that decision?" he asked softly.

She closed her eyes, sleep reaching out to claim her. "I never think much about being happy or unhappy. What's important is that Gracie is happy." With those words and Clay's arms wrapped tight around her, Libby fell asleep.

Monday morning started early with the usual routine. The car arrived at seven to pick them up for a day on the set.

For Clay, Sunday had been a workday. While Gracie

had been having voice and dance lessons, he'd been working Libby's computer, continuing the background checks on all the people that surrounded the two.

He'd worried that there would be some awkwardness between he and Libby after the night they'd shared together, but there had been none.

As the car took them to the studio, he thought about what Libby had shared with him just before she'd fallen asleep on Saturday night. In the darkness of the night, she'd shown him her vulnerability.

In her words, and in the tenor of her voice, he'd heard the cry of a little girl who'd wanted nothing more than to be considered special by cold, distant parents.

The insight into her made him understand her a little bit better, but it didn't change the fact that he thought she was making mistakes where Gracie was concerned. But sleeping with Libby didn't give him the right to tell her what he thought. Making love with Libby didn't give him license to butt into her life.

"Today I get to swing on a rope and save my friends from the wicked uncle Jasper," Gracie said as the car pulled up to the movie studio gates.

"Swing on a rope? Sounds exciting," Clay replied.

"When Jordan told me about it, I was scared, but we practiced and it's really not scary at all," Gracie explained.

"She'll be fine. I'll be the one having a heart attack while they film the scene," Libby said with a laugh.

At that moment the car pulled to a halt and they got out and went inside where Gracie went directly to makeup and Clay and Libby took their usual seats in the area for the parents.

"I hear today is the day little Gracie gets to play hero," Marlene Baker said from just behind Clay. Clay clenched his jaw at the slightly catty tone in the woman's voice. He should be used to it. All the parents seemed to suffer a heady dose of cattiness when they spoke to each other.

"And I heard you-all had a little scare on Saturday." This time it was Richard who spoke from behind them.

Clay turned in his chair to look at the man. "And how did you hear that?"

Richard smiled. "There aren't many secrets in this town. The old grapevine is alive and well."

"It definitely gave us some tense moments," Libby said. "But all's well that ends well."

"I guess it's just a reminder that we always need to be vigilant when it comes to the safety of our kids," Richard said. "Especially in this line of work."

Clay said nothing, but what he wanted to ask was why parents would willfully place their children in a business that put them in the public eye, that made them potential targets for obsessed or mentally deranged people.

Had they forgotten what had happened to JonBenet Ramsey? Funny, he'd never considered the ramifications of a child star until now, until Gracie. It might be a fine lifestyle for some, but not for somebody he cared about. And whether he liked it or not, he cared about Gracie.

He reminded himself that he had no business worrying about what was right for Gracie. Although Libby had been soft and vulnerable on Saturday night, he knew she wouldn't welcome his thoughts on what was best for her daughter.

Everyone fell silent as the work for the day began. Clay watched Gracie perform, surprised at her level of professionalism, how easily she gave whatever Jordan asked of her.

When off-camera, her gaze went often to Libby, as if seeking reassurance. There was no denying the unbreak-able bond between Libby and her daughter. He suspected any man would have difficulty finding a place in Libby's heart when all the space was taken up with her intense love and ambition for her daughter.

When they broke for lunch, Clay, Libby and Gracie found themselves at a table with Richard and his daughter Kathryn. "I'm having a big birthday party next Saturday," Kathryn said to Gracie. "You have to come because you're my very best friend."

Gracie turned to look at her mother and Libby looked at Clay. "Is there a problem?" Richard asked. "I know it's kind of last minute, but I thought Kathryn was going to be with her mother next weekend. That fell through so we're having a party, right, pumpkin?" He placed an arm around the red-haired girl and gave her a quick hug.

"You have to come, Gracie," Kathryn exclaimed. "I'm having clowns and pony rides and we're having it in the backyard."

"I was going to get out official invitations, but time got away from me so we're just inviting all the kids in the film and a few of Kathryn's other friends and their parents," Richard said.

"I don't see why we can't come," Libby said, then looked at Clay for confirmation.

A kids' party in a friend's backyard, surely that would be all right, he thought. He nodded his assent. As the two girls talked about what Kathryn might like as a birthday present, Clay smiled at Libby and tried not to think about the night they had shared together.

She was dressed for business today, in a tailored white blouse and navy slacks, but whenever he gazed at her all he could think about was how she'd looked naked and gasping his name.

Her eyes had been the deepest blue of midnight and she'd responded to him with a voracity that had stunned and delighted him.

He frowned as he thought about the conversation they'd had. She'd asked him if he'd ever had a passion, if he'd ever felt passionate about anything. It had surprised him to realize he hadn't.

He'd always known his place in life, had always known he'd go to work for the family business. He'd never felt the passion she'd talked about, had never wanted for anything except what life brought his way.

They had just finished lunch and Richard and Kathryn had already left when Charlie Wheeler appeared, his broad face wreathed in a smile as he approached where they sat.

"There you are," he said. "I thought I'd drop in and see

how my favorite client is doing." He patted the top of Gracie's head.

"I'm going to a birthday party next Saturday," Gracie announced.

"That's good. Birthday parties are always lots of fun." He directed his attention to Libby. "Heard you had a little excitement on Saturday."

"A little," Libby replied.

Clay didn't bother to ask how Gracie's agent had heard what happened. As Richard had said, the grapevine was alive and well in Hollywood.

"Well, just thought I'd drop by and check in." He snapped his fingers and reached inside his suit jacket pocket. "Almost forgot." He looked at Clay as he pulled out a photo. "I hunted down an old picture of your father when we worked on that film together years ago. Thought you might like to have it."

Clay took the photo from him. "Thanks, I appreciate it." He glanced at the picture of seven men standing in a row. It took him only a second to recognize his father. Red stood in the center, tall and broad-shouldered. He stuck the photo in his shirt pocket to look at more closely later.

Minutes later he and Libby once again took their seats to watch the remainder of the filming for the day. The set had been transformed to appear like a heavily wooded area.

Although Clay thought the whole thing looked fake and cheesy, Libby explained to him that computer images would be added in later to make it appear real.

Gracie appeared on a platform about ten feet in the air and the rest of the children stood in a group on a platform across the stage. Gracie smiled brightly and waved to Clay and Libby.

"She doesn't look scared," he said.

"She's practiced it half a dozen times," Libby said. "All she has to do is hang on and swing across. She's made it each time she's done it."

Clay was relieved to see that in the center of the stage they had laid down a large, air-filled cushion. If her hands slipped halfway through the swing and she fell, at least she wouldn't get badly hurt.

Still, Clay's stomach muscles clenched as Gracie got into position on the ledge. She looked so tiny, but he'd watched her work out with her trainer and knew her little arms were strong.

"Okay people, I want quiet on the set," Jordan roared. "We want to get this in a single take so our little star doesn't get too tired."

As people scrambled for positions and Jordan shouted instructions, Libby surprised him by reaching for his hand. She cast him a nervous smile as he squeezed her cold, slender fingers.

It surprised him that she'd reached out to him, that she'd reached out to anyone. He was certain that the woman he'd met when he'd first arrived at the house would have never sought reassurance from another human being.

Somehow in the last week he'd not only managed to get into her bed, but he'd apparently managed to gain her trust. He knew it for what it was, a gift from a woman who rarely gave such gifts of herself.

"Okay," Jordan yelled. "And action!"

The scene began with the children on the far ledge wondering who was going to save them, how they were going to be rescued. Malcolm cried that they were all going to die and Kathryn angrily told him to shut up, that somehow, some way, help would come.

The dialogue went without a hitch, each child playing their roles to perfection. When it came time for Gracie to swing to the rescue from the ten-foot-high ledge, she said a line of dialogue and grabbed the vinelike rope.

As her feet left the platform she plunged straight downward, her body crashing onto the floor just shy of the air cushion.

Chapter 9

Stunned silence.

"Cut! Jesus," Jordan exclaimed.

Libby bolted from her seat, her heart crashing against her ribs as she raced toward her baby. Gracie lay in a crumple, the length of rope on top of her.

Libby was vaguely aware of activity around her as she knelt next to Gracie, tears blurring her vision. A wave of relief tore through her as she saw that Gracie was conscious.

"Mommy, my ankle hurts." Gracie started to sit up.

"Don't move, honey," Clay said, his voice thick and unsteady. "Just lie there until the medics get here and check you out."

"Does anything else hurt besides your ankle?" Libby asked.

"I don't know." Tears filled Gracie's eyes. "That was too scary."

Definitely too scary, Libby thought.

Jordan was busy screaming orders at anyone and everyone, his face a taut mask. The other parents and children crowded around Gracie.

Within minutes two medics arrived with a stretcher. They carefully transferred Gracie to the stretcher, then started for the door where an ambulance awaited to take her to the hospital.

"You go on," Clay said to Libby. "I'll meet you at the hospital in a little while."

She nodded, barely taking in his words as she hurried to follow Gracie into the waiting ambulance. Although Gracie wasn't crying and didn't appear to be seriously hurt, Libby wouldn't rest easy until she was thoroughly checked out by a doctor.

"My hands didn't slip, Mommy," Gracie said once they were loaded into the ambulance and on their way to the hospital. "The rope didn't hold me." She caught her lower lip with her bottom teeth. "Am I in trouble?"

"Oh, no, baby, you didn't do anything wrong," Libby assured her.

"Is Jordan going to be mad at me?"

"Nobody is going to be mad at you," Libby said firmly. "It wasn't your fault."

"My ankle really hurts," Gracie said.

The medic, an attractive blonde who had identified herself as Kate checked Gracie's ankle. "It's swelling up.

There's no way to know if it's broken or not without an X-ray, but in the meantime I'll put an ice pack on it."

Libby held Gracie's hand as Kate applied the pack. By that time they were pulling up to the hospital's emergency entrance.

There were definite advantages to being a Hollywood golden child. Instead of sitting in an overcrowded waiting room with other sick or injured people, they were whisked into a private examination room immediately upon arrival.

Within minutes Dr. John Sanchez was examining Gracie and listening to exactly what had happened. "I'll send her up to X-ray for that ankle. She must have taken the brunt of the fall there. Otherwise, she seems to be fine except for some bumps and bruises. Unfortunately, X-ray is backed up right now so you might have to wait a little while."

"That's fine," Libby replied as waves of relief coursed through her. If the worst injury was Gracie's ankle and a few bruises, then she could live with that. Thank God she hadn't landed on her head or broken her back.

They had been in the examination room for almost an hour when the technicians came to wheel Gracie to X-ray. Libby was instructed to remain where she was and told that Gracie would be back in just a few minutes.

She sank into one of the two chairs in the examining room and tried to still the racing beat of her heart. She closed her eyes, but in her mind she played and replayed that moment when Gracie's feet had left the ledge and she'd plunged straight to the floor.

The sickening sound of her hitting the floor echoed again and again in Libby's head. It was supposed to have been a relatively easy stunt. Gracie had practiced it several times without any problems. So what had happened this time? What had gone wrong?

As the rush of adrenaline that had filled her from the moment of Gracie's impact slowly ebbed away, she began to tremble. How close they had come to tragedy. How close she had come to losing everything she held dear.

She knew kids had accidents all the time. They fell out of trees or off bicycles. They broke arms or cut knees. But this was the first time Gracie had ever been really hurt.

She told herself that this could have happened anywhere, that these kinds of accidents happened every day. It just so happened that Gracie's accident had taken place on the set of a movie.

Wrapping her arms around her shoulders, she tried to still the cold trembling that had taken possession of her body. From other examining rooms she heard the sounds of moaning, of children crying and the soft murmur of voices.

Where was Clay? Why hadn't he come with them? What could he be doing at the studio that was taking so long?

She frowned and stood. It was crazy, but for just a moment she thought she needed Clay. For just a brief instance, she yearned for his arms to hold her tight, she wanted to lean into his broad, strong chest.

But that was ridiculous. Libby didn't need anyone. She'd learned from her childhood not to need, not to want anyone to be there for her. She'd learned a long time ago that she was strong enough to be alone and one sexy, cowboy bodyguard wasn't about to change that.

She wasn't sure how long she'd sat staring at the walls when finally Gracie was wheeled back into the room. "The X-ray didn't hurt at all," she exclaimed. Her smile went a long way to ease Libby's worries.

Almost immediately Dr. Sanchez reappeared. "Well, the good news is the ankle isn't broken," he said. "The bad news is she has a sprain. We'll wrap it up and she should stay off it as much as possible for the next week or so."

Jordan wouldn't be happy with that news, she thought. Oh well, he'd just have to spend the next week shooting scenes that didn't involve Gracie.

At that moment Clay arrived. Even though he greeted Gracie with a smile and a soft, calming voice, his eyes were turbulent with suppressed emotion and his muscles were taut.

Libby tensed, wondering what had happened at the studio after she and Gracie had left. But she didn't want to question him while Gracie was present.

"I got a sprained ankle, Mr. Clay," Gracie said.

"I'm sorry to hear that." He walked over and swept a strand of Gracie's hair away from her forehead, his smile as gentle as Libby had ever seen.

"But I'm not going to cry because cowboys are tough," Gracie said bravely.

"I'll send in a nurse to wrap that ankle, then we'll get you people out of here," Dr. Sanchez said.

An hour later they arrived home. Libby was eager to talk to Clay about what happened at the studio after she and Gracie had left, but for the remainder of the afternoon and early evening she had no opportunity to talk to him alone.

By the time Gracie was asleep, Libby was exhausted. Her daughter had been a demanding patient throughout the evening, showing a cranky side that told Libby the ankle was more painful than Gracie pretended.

She left Gracie's bedroom and breathed a sigh of relief. She felt as if she'd scarcely had time to process what had happened and all that needed to be done with Gracie laid up for a week.

She met Clay in the hallway, his features set in taut lines. "We need to talk," he said. As she followed him down the stairs, she suddenly didn't want to hear what he had to say. She was afraid of what he had to tell her.

When they reached the living room she went directly to the bar. "I think after the day I've had, I deserve a drink."

"You'd better make it a double."

Libby frowned and splashed two jiggers of gin into the bottom of a glass. She added a liberal dose of tonic, then topped it with a slice of lime.

"Mind making me one of those?"

It must be bad news if Clay was having a drink, she thought. She fixed a second gin and tonic, then handed it to him. She carried hers to the sofa and sank down. She took a deep drink, then looked up at him. "What happened after we left the set this afternoon?"

Clay sat next to her and again she fought the impulse to lean into him, to gain strength from his presence. Instead she took another drink and felt the bite of the gin warm her insides.

"After you left I examined the rope and what I discovered was that it looked like somebody had cut through it except for a few strands."

She stared at him blankly, for a moment unable to make sense of his words. The rope had been cut? Surely he was mistaken. "Are you sure?" Even as the words left her mouth she knew he would never have said anything if he wasn't sure.

His jaw muscles pulsed as he held her gaze intently. "That rope was cut so that it wouldn't have held the weight of a small cat."

The warmth that the gin had produced chilled as she realized the implication of his words. "So somebody wanted Gracie to fall." Her mouth was so dry she had to force the words out.

He nodded and a wind of icy air blew through Libby. Somebody had tried to hurt Gracie. It was an evil thing, to cut through the rope, to know that the result would be a fall that might seriously harm her.

Tears blurred her eyes as exhaustion mingled with fear. For the first time in years she felt herself falling apart and she couldn't do anything to stop it.

Clay took her drink from her hand, set both his and hers on the coffee table, then leaned forward and gathered her into his arms.

Although she had told herself over and over again that she didn't need anyone, that she didn't need Clay, she dropped her head to his chest as several sobs ripped from the depths of her.

She'd been able to convince herself that the letters weren't a real threat, that whoever was writing them lived far away and posed no real danger. But there was no way to rationalize the cut rope away.

Clay held her tight and the feel of his arms surrounding her broke loose a dam of emotion she hadn't known she possessed. She wept as she hadn't since she'd been a child.

The difference was when she'd cried as a child it had been in the darkness of her room, with no arms to hold her, nobody to soothe away the tears.

Clay murmured into her hair, noises to comfort but without any real meaning. Even if he'd spoken words that meant something at the moment, she wouldn't have been able to process anything.

She cried until there was nothing left inside her except the fear for her daughter and the overwhelming embarrassment of her breakdown. Still, she remained in his embrace, her face shoved against the clean scent of his short-sleeved cotton dress shirt, reluctant to leave the warmth of his strong arms.

His hand stroked her hair and she kept her eyes closed, wanting nothing more than to sleep and wake up and find out that this was all just a terrible nightmare.

But she knew there was no awakening from this nightmare, that no matter how long she slept this wasn't going to just disappear. Somebody wanted to hurt her child.

She finally wiped her eyes, then raised her head to look at him. "I'm sorry. I can't believe I just did that."

"What? Acted human?" He crooked a dark brow wryly. "Don't apologize for that." He released his hold on her as she sat up.

"So, what happens now?" She worried a hand through her hair, her thoughts scattered.

"I told Jordan that Gracie wouldn't be back to work until a full investigation was done on what happened with that rope and who might be responsible."

Libby frowned, unsure what she thought about him taking such measures without consulting her. Still, it was difficult to be angry with the one person she knew was on her side, the one person who was on Gracie's side. "What did he say about that?"

"He agreed and promised to get to the bottom of things as soon as possible. I think the fall scared him almost as much as it scared us."

"It only scared him because if Gracie became unable to finish the film it would cost Jordan millions of dollars," she said.

Clay picked up his drink and took a swallow, then set it down once again. "I also contacted a Detective Holt. He met me at the studio and now the investigation of the fall and the letters are in his hands."

Libby stood, anger surging inside her. "You should have consulted me before you did that." He had no idea of the ramifications of just such an action. He was an outsider to the Hollywood scene and couldn't know.

"And if I'd consulted you, what would you have said to do?" He didn't pause long enough to let her reply. "Libby, I told you when I first arrived that I'm a bodyguard, not an investigator."

He stood and took a step toward her. "And that private investigator that you hired came up with nothing." He took another step forward, bringing him close enough to her that she could see the flecks of gold in his green eyes, feel his body heat radiating toward her. "Somebody wanted to hurt Gracie. There's no way to mistake what happened today on the set. It wasn't just an accident. It was attempted murder."

His words crashed through her and nearly brought her to her knees. Attempted murder. Those two words blew an icy chill through her and her knees buckled. She might have fallen had he not taken one step more and caught her in his arms.

"Surely not," she protested weakly. "The ledge wasn't that high." He was overreacting, talking about murder, she thought in desperation.

"That ledge was high enough that if she'd fallen wrong, she could have died. In my book that makes it attempted murder."

Tears once again blurred her vision as she looked up at him. "I just…I can't understand any of this. Why would anyone want to hurt her? She's just a little girl. She doesn't pose a threat to anyone."

"I know," he murmured into her hair as he held her tight against him. "I know, and I'll do everything in my power to see that nobody hurts her." He placed his palms on either side of her face. "You're exhausted. You need to get a good night's sleep."

"Sleep with me." She hadn't intended to say any such thing, but the moment the words left her mouth she knew that's what she wanted.

She wanted him beside her in bed, holding her and keeping nightmares at bay. For the first time in her life, she needed somebody and that somebody was Clay.

Clay walked with Libby up the stairs toward her bedroom. He knew she hadn't invited him into her bed for lovemaking, but rather because she was afraid.

He'd seen the fear that had darkened her eyes, felt the trembling of her body when he'd held her, and he could do nothing but try to assure her that he'd do whatever he could to protect Gracie. And hold her if she needed to be held.

They didn't speak a word when they reached her room. She disappeared into the bathroom and he moved to the window to stare outside and tried to process all that had happened that afternoon.

He closed his eyes as the memory of Gracie falling replayed itself. The sound of her body hitting the floor had caused his heart to plunge to his feet. Never in all of his years had he known such terror.

If anything happened to Gracie, he wasn't sure how

he'd survive. Her little face would forever be in his heart, the sound of her laughter would haunt him until the day he died.

He knew Libby had been irritated that he'd called in the detective, but he had to do his job the way he saw fit and it had been time to call in help. Anonymous letters were one thing, the fall on the set had been quite another. It had been time to bring in the cops, and image and publicity be damned.

Still facing the window, he began to unbutton his shirt. It was then that he remembered the photo that Charlie had given him at lunch that day. He pulled it from his pocket and walked closer to the lamp on the nightstand.

As he stared at the image of his father, a wealth of homesickness filled him. Although after their mother's murder Red had gone through a spell of drinking too much and being distant with his kids, he'd eventually come around to be one hell of a father.

Even though there'd been five kids vying for his attention, he'd always managed to make each and every one of them feel special.

He frowned as he studied the faces of the other men in the picture. One of the other men looked more than just a little bit familiar. He looked like a younger, thinner Jim Ramsey. Ramsey was the sheriff in Cotter Creek.

He flipped the photo over, pleased to see the men's names written on the back. Sure enough, there it was. Jimmy Ramsey. Odd, that his father had never mentioned that Ramsey had once worked with him in Hollywood.

He looked up at the sound of the bathroom door creaking open. Libby stood hesitantly in the doorway, clad in a light pink silk nightgown.

For a woman he'd thought to be a ball buster when he'd first laid eyes on her, she looked achingly fragile with a pulse beating visibly in the hollow of her throat and her hand trembling as it swept through her hair.

"Would you rather I go to my own room?" he asked softly, wondering if she'd changed her mind about him sleeping in here with her.

"No. No, I need you here." She dropped her hand from her hair and started to turn down the bed. She kept her gaze from his, as if her need to have him near was something shameful.

He walked over to her and took her by her upper arms, forcing her to look into his face. "You know, Libby, there's nothing wrong with needing someone."

She raised her chin a notch, her eyes firing darkly. "I've never needed anyone in my life."

"Are you sure that's a strength and not a weakness?" He raked a finger down her jawline. She was the most complicated woman he'd ever known and she raised complicated emotions inside him. He dropped his hand. "Let's get some sleep."

Within minutes they were side-by-side in the king-size bed, the room dark and silent except for the sound of her breathing.

She moved closer to him, close enough that he knew she wanted him to hold her. He obliged, wrapping an arm around her shoulder and pulling her closer against the length of his body.

He tried to ignore the warmth of her curves, the feminine scent of her that eddied in the air. The last thing he wanted to do was to allow himself to become physically stirred by her nearness.

Instead he focused on contemplating what the next day would bring. The detective was supposed to get in touch with him sometime tomorrow to let him know how the investigation into the cut rope was going. Clay knew the problem would be that too many people had access to the set.

He also wanted to finish checking into the backgrounds of the people who were working on the film. So far he'd managed to get through more than half of them, but nothing yet had sent up red flags of warning.

One thing was clear. Whoever had cut that rope knew Gracie, at least on a casual level. That meant the letters might also be coming from somebody familiar to either Gracie or Libby.

He'd neglected to ask Libby if she had any enemies in this town of smoke and mirrors. Although everyone on the set seemed to like her, he had to remember that this was a town of actors and actresses, and what you saw was not necessarily how it was.

Perhaps Libby had made an enemy who was trying to hurt her by going through Gracie. He frowned. It had been stupid of him not to ask her from the very beginning if she had pissed somebody off.

All thoughts of who might be mad at her fled from his mind as she turned over in his arms and pressed her lips into the hollow of his throat.

His response was instantaneous. Every muscle in his body tensed and fire licked in his veins. He didn't move, unsure what she had in mind, although the feel of her mouth against his skin had definitely put an idea in his mind.

Her mouth moved to the underside of his jaw and he wondered if she had any idea what she was doing to him. "Libby." Her name was not just a whisper, but a definite warning.

"I want you to make love to me, Clay." Her words were whispered but held a yearning as strong as a shout.

"I'd be happy to oblige you." He moved his head so he could capture her lips with his own. Her hungry response nearly stole his breath away.

It had been that way the first time he'd kissed her and he wondered if he kissed her for the rest of his life if each kiss would be as exciting as the last. Somehow he thought so.

Something about this woman excited him as no other had done in his life. The scent of her, the feel of her skin, the taste of her lips all combined to electrify him in a way that was both foreign and wonderfully right.

Where before when they had made love he'd tried to take his time, wanting to give her as much pleasure as possible, he now sensed in her the need to be fast and frantic, to unleash passion unchecked and take her without finesse. She didn't want to be taken sweetly, she wanted an out-of-body, out-of-her-mind experience.

He kissed her almost savagely and she welcomed it, raking her fingers down his back and gasping with pleasure. He tore his mouth from hers and sat up only long enough to pull off his boxers and fumble for his wallet on the nightstand.

In the darkness he could hear the faint hiss of silk leaving her body as he quickly put on a condom. When he took her into his arms once again she was naked and wild.

He let her take the lead and suspected he was little more than a tool for a release of emotions she didn't know how to handle. But that was fine with him, for as she straddled him, he was more than ready for her.

She sank down on him and for a moment lay on his chest, her face buried in the hollow of his neck. He stroked her hair and tried to maintain control while buried deep inside her.

He'd be finished in a minute if he allowed himself to focus on the press of her full breasts against his chest and her tight, moist heat enveloping him.

Then she rose up and moved her hips against his, and a deep groan issued forth from him. He allowed her to ride him until he could stand it no longer, then he pushed her onto her back and took her until he was mindless with her.

He was vaguely aware of her crying out his name, then shuddering with the force of her release. That sent him over the edge and he stiffened as his own climax left him breathless and weak.

He rolled off her and to the side, feeling as boneless as a fish fillet. He turned his head to look at her, but the darkness in the room prevented him from seeing her features.

She took in deep breaths, then released a low, sexy laugh. "You sure know how to make a woman forget her troubles for a little while."

"I aim to please."

He sensed her rolling over onto her side to face him. "Do you do this often? Have sex with a client?"

"Never. I made it a rule a long time ago never to mix business with pleasure. You're the first client to make me break my own rule."

"Sometimes it's good to break the rules."

He smiled. "In this particular instance, it was more than good. I'll be right back." He got up and padded into the bathroom.

When he returned to the bed she was once again wearing her nightgown. He wrapped an arm around her and she leaned into him, her heart a steady rhythm against his own.

They remained that way a long time and he thought she'd fallen asleep. He frowned into the darkness, wondering what in the hell he was doing.

He shouldn't be here in her bed. He shouldn't be holding her close to his heart, smelling the scent that stirred him on a million levels. He couldn't lose sight of his job here and the fact that eventually this job would end.

She was a Hollywood kind of woman and he was an

Oklahoma kind of man. She wanted fame and fortune for her daughter and if he had any say in it he would want something very different for Gracie. There would never be, could never be, anything between them except this temporary Hollywood kind of affair.

She stirred against him and released a deep, weary sigh. "Clay. She's all I have."

The words were barely audible, but filled with the deep, hollow fear of a mother for her only child. He tightened his arm around her, his heart clenching with her vulnerability. "I know," he replied, wishing he could say something that would take away her fear.

Chapter 10

Clay came awake with a start, his heart pounding anxiously. A dream. No, not just a dream, rather it had been a nightmare. He sucked in a deep breath to steady himself as the haunting vision replayed in his mind.

Gracie had been gone and Libby had been weeping, begging him to do something, to find her baby because Gracie was her life, her reason for being.

The worst part of the nightmare had been the overwhelming helplessness that had filled him as he realized he didn't know where to look for Gracie.

A whisper of dawn light crept in through the curtains. He turned his head to see Libby sleeping next to him, her features barely discernible in the faint glow of the room.

Even in sleep she was beautiful, but he couldn't help

remembering the torment that had ridden her features in his dream, the agony that had darkened her eyes as she'd begged him to find Gracie.

He frowned and slid out of bed, careful not to awaken her. He pulled on his jeans, grabbed his shirt and things from the nightstand, then crept out of her room and into his own.

A brisk shower washed away any lingering thought of his nightmare. He dressed in a clean pair of jeans and a T-shirt and headed down to the kitchen for some coffee.

Helen sat at the table, the morning paper in front of her. She frowned as he entered the kitchen. In the days that he'd been in the house he'd grown accustomed to her sour nature.

"Morning Helen." He went to the cabinet and pulled out a coffee mug.

"Ms. Libby isn't going to think it's such a good morning," she said with the faintest hint of satisfaction in her voice.

"Why is that?" He poured himself a cup of coffee then joined her at the table.

"See for yourself." She shoved the paper, a daily movie industry tabloid, in front of him.

Close Call For America's Littlest Sweetheart.

He swallowed a groan at the headline and quickly scanned the article. A close source had told the reporter about Gracie's accident. It was all there: the cut rope, the fact that detectives had been brought in and the news that the movie would halt production while Gracie recovered from her fall.

The article even mentioned the brick through the window of the little star's bedroom and the reporter also added a side note on Hollywood stalking and the dangers of being in the public eye.

The last thing Libby had wanted was any publicity and Clay had a feeling she was going to be livid when she saw this article, which was definitely slanted to indicate somebody wanted to hurt Gracie Bryant.

He shoved the paper back toward Helen, a headache blossoming in the center of his forehead. "Terrible thing," Helen said. "Little girls shouldn't have to worry about somebody trying to hurt them or working their childhood away."

He glanced at her sharply. "You don't approve of Gracie's career?"

"As far as I'm concerned, show business eats little children alive." A flash of pain darkened her eyes and she got up from the table. "You read the tabloids and they're full of stories of maladjusted child stars who get into drugs and drink, and never really adjust to real life."

Clay watched as she pulled a tray of freshly baked biscuits out of the oven. He rubbed his forehead and stared out the window where the sun had fully peaked over the horizon.

There was apparently more to Helen than her pots and pans. What did she do all day when Libby, Gracie and he left for the studio? She obviously didn't approve of Gracie's work.

Did she have something to do with the letters Gracie

had received? Was it possible she or somebody she knew had been at the studio yesterday intent on creating an accident that would get everyone's attention?

He raked a hand through his hair with a sigh of frustration. He was losing it, suspecting an old woman of dastardly deeds. Still, there had been something in her eyes that had piqued his interest, a flash of what had appeared to be grief. He hadn't checked into her background too intensely as Libby had assured him she'd come with impeccable references. He now made a mental note to do a little more digging into her background.

But first, he wanted to call home. He finished his coffee, then headed back up the stairs to his bedroom. It was just after six-thirty and he knew his father would be awake and probably drinking his morning coffee with Smokey.

He grabbed his cell phone, punched in the numbers for home, then sank down onto the edge of his bed. Red answered, his pleasure obvious as he heard the sound of Clay's voice. "How are things going out there?"

"Frustrating," Clay replied honestly, and quickly filled his father in on what had happened so far. "But that's not why I'm calling. I met an old acquaintance of yours."

"Who?"

"Charlie Wheeler. He's Gracie's agent and wields a lot of power in this town."

Red chuckled. "Good old Charlie. I'm not surprised. He was always too smart and too ambitious to stay a stuntman forever."

"He gave me an old photo yesterday. It was of all the

stuntmen who worked on *The Devil's Run*. Why didn't you tell me Sheriff Ramsey had worked with you in Hollywood?"

"I don't know. It never came up. Your mother and I had been here in Cotter Creek for about a year when Jim called and told me he wanted out of Hollywood. He asked me how we liked Cotter Creek. We told him we loved it here and six weeks later he showed up in town. It was a long time ago, Clay."

"I was just curious. So, how are things going there?" He listened as his father told him the latest family and town news and again he was filled with a wave of homesickness.

"Have you heard that Joshua is coming home?" Red asked.

"I spoke with him last week and he said he was seriously considering leaving the big city behind and heading back to the ranch."

"I heard from him yesterday and he put in his two weeks' notice at his job. Said he hoped to be back here within a month."

"It will be good to have him back home," Clay said. "Hopefully by the time Joshua gets there, I'll be back, too. When this particular job is over, I need some downtime."

There was a long pause. "You doing okay, son?" Red's voice was filled with concern.

"Yeah, it's just that this one is getting to me more than a little bit. I can't seem to get a handle on who's posing the threats and I don't know what I'll do if something happens to Gracie."

"You know how important it is to stay objective, to keep detached from your clients," Red said softly.

"Yeah, I know." And it's too late for that, Clay thought ruefully. "It's just hard to stay detached when your client is a little girl with big blue eyes and a smile that lights up the sky." He didn't even want to mention how difficult it was to remain detached from Libby.

"Take care, Clay. You know you're just a temporary fix. When the danger passes, they'll move on with their lives."

"Don't worry, I'm not about to lose sight of that." The two men visited for a little while longer, then Clay told his father goodbye and they hung up.

He got up from the bed and moved to the window to stare outside. The sprinkler system came to life, misting the perfectly manicured lawn and gardens.

A foul mood was descending on him, a foul mood bred in frustration and the knowledge that he'd gotten himself in too deep with Libby Bryant. He'd known better than to sleep with her the first time.

He'd always prided himself on the fact that he maintained self-control in all areas in his life, but something about Libby made him forget self-control. He was in too deep and that definitely irritated him.

"Did you see the paper?"

He turned from the window to see Libby standing in his doorway, the offending paper clutched tightly in her hand. She practically vibrated with anger.

"Yeah, I saw it."

She stepped into the room and began to pace in front

of the foot of his bed. "How did this happen? Who talked to a reporter and made my daughter's life front-page news?" She glared at him as if he were personally responsible for the item in the paper. Her anger only fed the irritation that had taken root inside him.

"You people make me laugh," he said dryly. He moved away from the window and stood at the foot of his bed.

She stopped pacing and frowned. "'You people'? What does that mean?"

"You movie star people. You people who put yourselves in the public eye, court the media when it serves your purpose, then slug the paparazzi who take a bad picture or cuss the reporter who writes an unflattering story."

Her eyes narrowed. "You don't know anything about it. You have no idea how things work here."

"Yeah, and I'm not sure I want to know," he said thinly. "I know this much, you put your daughter out there for every molester and mentally ill person in the world to see, then get upset when some creep fixates on her. You can't have it both ways, Libby. You say you aren't a stage mother, but you're living your dreams, healing your childhood miseries, through her."

He was out of control and he knew it, but suddenly he was angry. Angry with himself for not being able to figure out who wanted to hurt Gracie and angry with Libby for placing her daughter in a position to be in danger.

"You're worried about bad publicity when somebody is trying to hurt your daughter. You're afraid this is going to queer a new movie deal or ruin an opportunity for an endorsement when what you should be worried about is Gracie's well-being."

She gasped, her cheeks turning red as if he'd physically slapped her face. "How dare you speak to me that way."

He grinned without humor. "Oh, yeah. I forgot that in this town speaking the truth is frowned upon. Everybody sucks up to Libby Bryant so they can get a piece of her pretty, talented daughter."

"You have no idea what you're talking about," she retorted. "I'm not living out my dreams through Gracie. This is her dream. She loves what she does."

"Jesus, Libby, she doesn't know anything different," he countered. "Gracie is a people pleaser and all she knows is that when she acts it makes you happy. She loves acting because she knows that's what you want her to do. You've had her in this business since she was old enough to talk. She's not old enough to have any dreams of her own, so don't fool yourself."

Her mouth opened then closed and she turned on her heels and left his room. Clay stood staring at where she'd stood, wondering what in the hell had just happened.

He'd lost it. It was as simple as that. He'd been hateful, but everything he'd said had been what he'd thought from the moment he'd arrived and met little Gracie. This was not a life he'd ever want for his kid.

He was worried about getting in too deep with Libby. He had a feeling he didn't have to worry about that anymore. In fact, after what had just happened it was very possible he'd be sent packing and on his way home by evening.

He wasn't sure whether that possibility filled him with relief or despair.

Libby stood in her bedroom, trembling with anger. How dare he? How dare he say the hateful things he'd said to her? He was nothing but a stupid cowboy from some podunk town. What did he know about her life? What did he know about Gracie's dreams? What did he know about this business or this town?

She sank down onto the edge of her bed, afraid her trembling knees would hold her no longer. In a fit of temper she flung the newspaper across the room, where it fluttered in pieces to the floor.

Tears filled her eyes and she tried to tell herself they were tears of rage, but it was more than that. There was a tiny piece deep inside her that was afraid his words held some truth, but she refused to dig it out and examine it.

Instead she embraced the anger, just as she'd embraced the passion the night before. It was so much easier to feel those things than to allow the fear that niggled in the back of her mind to take hold.

At least now she knew what Clay really thought about her, that he thought she was a stage mother vicariously living through her daughter's talent and successes. He thought that she was sacrificing her daughter to achieve her own dreams.

There was no way he'd ever understand that she'd just

wanted to be the kind of mother she'd never had, that she'd sacrificed her own life for Gracie's dreams.

She got up off the bed and retrieved the newspaper she'd flung moments before. She read the article once again, then set it on the nightstand and left the bedroom. No point crying over spilt milk.

Clay West didn't have to understand the forces that drove her or agree with the decisions she made for herself and her daughter. He was hired help and nothing more. She'd been momentarily weak where he was concerned, but that wouldn't happen again. From this moment forward their relationship would be strictly business.

Never again would she indulge herself in needing anyone. She knew better and the brief lapse in judgment where Clay was concerned wouldn't be an issue in the future.

The three of them had just suffered through a tense, silent breakfast when the buzzer indicated somebody at the front gate. The visitor identified himself as Detective Holt. Libby buzzed him in, then called Molly to take Gracie up to her room.

"Come on, Gracie. You can practice your lines with me for when you go back to work." Molly put an arm around Gracie to help her up the stairs as the doorbell rang to announce the detective.

Detective Harry Holt was a caricature of a Hollywood detective from a bad movie. Overweight, unkempt and smelling like the burning end of a cigar, he bumbled into the living room with a beatific smile on his face.

"Ms. Bryant, it's a pleasure to meet you." He held a beefy hand toward her.

"Nice meeting you, too," she said, and shook his slightly sweaty hand. "Please, have a seat." She gestured him toward her sofa.

"Mr. West." He nodded to Clay as he sank down and pulled a small notebook out of his shirt pocket. "I'm here about the incident at the movie studio yesterday." He flipped open the notebook and leaned forward, looking as if he might tumble head over heels off his perch on the edge of the sofa.

"Did you find out anything? Who was responsible?" Libby asked, her heart's rhythm stepping up in pace.

"No, nothing yet. I came by just to ask a few follow-up questions. By the way, how's the little one?"

"She's fine. Thankfully she just suffered a sprained ankle." Libby sank down in the chair opposite the detective.

Clay stood nearby, his features stoic, as they had been since their morning fight.

"Ms. Bryant, I was wondering if you know of anyone who might be angry with you, somebody who might try to hurt you through your daughter?"

Libby looked at Detective Holt in surprise. She'd never considered such a thing. Her automatic response was a definitive no, but she took a moment to consider the question thoughtfully. "I can't think of anyone who might be angry with me, but in this town you make enemies fairly easily."

"Speaking of enemies, Jordan Rutherford has made

more than his share in his years of working in this town," Detective Holt replied. "Three months ago a disturbed actor who Rutherford had nixed for a role in a movie broke into Rutherford's house and confronted him with a knife."

"Oh, my God." Libby gasped. "What happened?"

Holt scratched the side of his nose with the end of his pen. "Rutherford managed to talk the young man into giving up the knife by promising him another audition. As soon as the young man left, Rutherford called us. We picked up the actor and he spent a night in jail before he was bailed."

Holt scratched the other side of his nose, then continued. "My point is, we're also working the angle that it might be somebody who wants to hurt Rutherford."

"Why would somebody go after Gracie to hurt Jordan?" Clay asked.

Holt shrugged his massive shoulders. "She's his star. If she gets hurt, the production shuts down, he goes over budget and his reputation gets shredded."

"So what do you suggest we do?" Libby frowned.

"Stay vigilant. Keep an eye out for anything or anyone that doesn't look right. We'll be checking into the backgrounds of the people who are working on the film."

"Mr. West has already done some of that," Libby said.

Holt shot a sharp look at Clay. "Really? Have you found anything interesting?"

"No red flags in those I've checked," Clay replied.

"You'll let me know if something comes up?"

"Certainly," Clay agreed.

Holt looked back at Libby. "Mr. West mentioned yesterday that your daughter had received some nasty mail. I'd like to take it with me, see if our experts can pull any prints and check them against our database."

"Certainly, I'll just go get them." Libby rose and went into her office. The original letters had been returned to her from the private investigator she'd hired and were in a clear plastic bag in her desk drawer.

She sat at the desk and opened the drawer to retrieve the bag. She remained seated for a moment as the murmur of the men's voices drifted in from the living room. It wasn't even noon yet and she was already emotionally exhausted.

The argument with Clay had affected her far more deeply than she'd initially thought. The fact that it didn't appear to have bothered him at all depressed her even more.

How could a man be so tender, so passionate, and harbor such bad thoughts about her? How could a man want a woman and dislike her at the same time?

Realizing she needed to get back to the living room, she grabbed the bag and got up. Detective Holt stood as she reentered the room and he took the bag from her.

"I'll stay in touch," he assured her. "If you think of anything that might help the investigation, let me know. I can see myself out." He nodded to both of them, then headed for the front door.

When he'd gone, an awkward silence sprang up between

Libby and Clay. He jammed his hands into his jeans' pockets, his features giving nothing of his inner thoughts away.

"I hadn't thought that all this might have something to do with Jordan," she said, needing to break the silence.

"We don't know for sure that it does yet," he replied.

Before she could answer him the buzzer at the front gate rang, announcing the arrival of yet another visitor. "Speak of the devil," she said as Jordan Rutherford announced himself.

Several moments later the director breezed through the front door and wrapped his arms around Libby with a dramatic flair. "Dear woman," he exclaimed as he released her. "How's our girl?"

He didn't wait for a reply, but instead began to pace the living room with manic energy. "God, I've been worried sick. Anything…anything you want, I'll do to assure her safety. We'll hire half a dozen bodyguards and every inch of the set will be searched before each shoot." He finally paused to drag in a breath.

"Sit down, Jordan. You're making me nervous," Libby said. He plopped down on the sofa and gazed at her expectantly. "Gracie is fine. She needs to stay off her feet for a couple of days."

"Of course. I can shoot around her for a couple of days," Jordan said.

"She doesn't go back to work until you can assure us that the conditions are safe," Clay said. Libby stiffened, resenting his interference even though she agreed with what he'd said.

"And that's what I'm here to do," Jordan replied. "I'll work around her for the rest of the week and first thing Monday morning I'll make sure there are people on the set whose only job is to keep Gracie safe. I'll do whatever necessary to get this film in the can and it just won't be the kind of success I want without our Gracie."

He jumped up off the sofa, as if unable to sit still any longer. He began to pace once again. "When we find out who is responsible for that rope being cut, I'll personally see that they never work in this town again. We'll press charges and make sure they spend the next couple of years working in a prison show.

"Dammit, Libby, whatever you do, don't pull her out of my film. That will not only destroy this project, but it will also seriously damage Gracie's career. We've both worked too hard for that to happen. We've only got a couple of weeks of filming left. The movie is almost finished. If you pull her out now, we'd have to start all over again."

A headache blossomed, squeezing Libby's temples like a vise. She rubbed a finger at her temple, wishing everyone would just go away and let her think.

She knew that no matter what decision she made about Gracie's immediate future somebody was going to be upset or disappointed in her. While that had never bothered her before, she found that it did bother her now.

"Look, Jordan," Clay said. "We'll get back to you later in the week concerning Gracie's schedule. Right now she needs to get well and back on her feet."

For the first time Libby was grateful for Clay's intervention. Her head pounded too painfully for her to try to make any decision at the moment.

"Fine. Okay, that's fine," Jordan replied. "I just wanted to come by and tell you how sorry I am that this happened and that we'll do whatever necessary to see the completion of the project."

"I'll see you out," Clay said in obvious dismissal.

As he walked Jordan to the front door, Libby sank deeper into the chair cushion and once again rubbed her forehead. She was still seated there when Clay returned to the room.

"Look, I might be nothing more than a cowboy from Oklahoma, but I know you can't just breach Gracie's contract and yank her from the film," he said. "That wouldn't hurt just Jordan and Gracie, but would also threaten the livelihood of everyone working on the film."

"You're right." She dropped her hand from her forehead. "I can't pull her from the film, but I will insist on Jordan hiring some people to assure Gracie's safety and to check the conditions on the set."

He nodded, his eyes dark and impossible to read. "Jordan just told me that he expects to wrap up the movie by next weekend. I'll stay on the job until the filming for the movie is finished, then I'm done here. If we haven't identified the source of the threat at that time, then I think it would be best if you hired somebody else in my place."

She stared at him a long moment. "All right," she said softly. She knew it was for the best, that by the time the filming was finished it would be more than time for them to say goodbye.

But as she looked at him she couldn't help feeling that she was losing something valuable, something she wouldn't realize she had until it was gone.

Chapter 11

"I'd like it if you stayed here and lived with us forever," Gracie said to Clay as he sat next to her bed.

It was just the two of them in the room. Libby had left to take a phone call. For the past three days, ever since the article about Gracie had appeared in the newspaper, the phone had rung incessantly.

Clay's heart constricted at Gracie's words and he struggled to find the right reply. Before he could do so, she rolled over on her side and took his hand in her little one.

"It's kind of like having a daddy, having you here." Her hand squeezed his tightly and he felt the pressure work up his arm and straight to his heart.

She released his hand and rolled over on her back, staring up at the ceiling. "Kathryn's lucky. She has a daddy who lives with her all the time. My mommy told me that my daddy didn't really want to be a daddy so he went away." She turned back to look at him. "I think you'd make a very good daddy."

The kid was killing him. Day by day, moment by moment with her smiles and her laughter and her little-girl exuberance for life, she was ripping out a piece of his heart that he knew he'd never get back.

He cleared his throat and leaned back in the chair, needing to distance himself from her sweet little-girl smell and the longing he sensed in her. "Maybe someday your mommy will marry a nice man who will be your daddy."

"Why couldn't you marry her?" Gracie yawned sleepily. "You could marry her and be my daddy and we could go live on your ranch and pick beans in Mr. Red's garden. Then Mr. Red would be Grandpa Red." She sighed and rubbed her eyes. "I'd like to have a grandpa. Kathryn's grandpa takes her to get ice cream and makes funny faces."

Red would love having a granddaughter like Gracie, Clay thought. His father had been ready for grandchildren for a long time. Even the irascible Smokey would find Gracie a delight.

He was grateful to realize that Gracie had fallen asleep and no reply from him was necessary. Despite the fact that he could now leave her, he remained seated in the chair in the semidarkness of the room.

In just a little over a week he'd be gone. The film would be finished and Gracie's safety at that point would fall into somebody else's hands.

He was surprised to discover that the thought of leaving caused thick emotion to press in on his chest. Gracie and her mother had left an indelible mark on his heart.

Before he left, he'd make sure that whoever was in charge of Gracie's safety was somebody reputable, somebody who could be trusted. There was no way he could walk away and leave her safety to chance.

But he had to walk away. The past week had been difficult. He and Libby had warily circled each other being overly polite and distant. It had been damned uncomfortable, especially since he still wanted her.

He drew in a deep breath and closed his eyes, for a moment thinking of his desire for Libby. The scent of her moved him, the hollow of her throat begged for kisses and her lush curves made him ache.

He liked so many things about her. She was sharp and intelligent, she had a wonderful sense of humor. He admired the love and devotion she displayed toward Gracie. She was everything he would want in a woman, except for the driving ambition that seemed to blind her to everything else in life.

He understood now the deep hole that had been left in her from her childhood. He could sympathize with the lack of love and support she'd suffered, but understanding and sympathizing didn't mean he could accept the decisions she now made.

"She asleep?" Libby's soft voice came from the doorway. He nodded and stood. He followed her out into the hallway.

"You want to have a nightcap with me?"

He looked at her in surprise. In the past couple of days she'd made no attempt to spend any time with him or have any real conversation with him. "All right," he agreed with a touch of wariness.

As he followed her down the stairs he wondered if she was hoping for an apology from him. If so, she'd be disappointed. He wouldn't apologize for what he'd said because he'd spoken from his beliefs, from his heart.

"That was Richard Walker who called," she said as she went to the bar and, obviously remembering what he'd drunk last time, grabbed the gin and tonic. "He said with Gracie not being on the set this week and with everything that was going on with her he wanted to remind us of Kathryn's birthday party tomorrow. He wanted to know if we were going to be there."

Clay moved to the opposite side of the bar from her and took the drink she offered him. "What did you tell him?"

She finished making her own drink and for the first time her gaze met his. "I told him I wasn't sure. Contrary to what you believe about me, I do care about Gracie's safety. I figured I'd leave the issue of attending the birthday party up to you."

"I never questioned that you care about Gracie," he replied. "I just don't agree…"

She held up a hand. "Please, Clay, I don't have the energy tonight to go over it all again. I was just wondering what we were going to do about the party."

For the first time he noticed that she did look exhausted.

Her blue eyes appeared faded in color and her features were drawn. Apparently the past week hadn't been any easier on her than it had been on him.

"Come on, let's sit," Clay said gently.

She came out from behind the bar and together they sat on the sofa. He wished he couldn't smell the scent of her perfume for the fragrance reminded him of how she'd felt in his arms, how crazy hot he'd been when he'd taken her.

He frowned and took a swallow of his drink, needing to will away the images in his mind and focus on the matter at hand.

Gracie had mentioned the party several times in the past week. Physically she was fine. The swelling in the ankle had all but disappeared and she was back to running full-tilt.

"She'll be disappointed if we don't go," he finally said.

"She can live with a little disappointment if necessary," Libby replied. "If you don't think it's safe, then we don't go. It's as simple as that."

No, nothing was as simple as that. Nothing about this entire case had been simple from the very beginning. He took another swallow of his drink and thought about the birthday party.

Richard had told them he was inviting the kids in the cast of the movie and that the party was taking place in his backyard.

Certainly Clay didn't believe any of the children were responsible for the threats against Gracie. The party should be relatively safe and Gracie would be so disappointed if she couldn't attend. He vaguely wondered when he'd become the kind of man who didn't want to disappoint a little girl.

"We'll go," he finally said. "It didn't sound like it was going to be an extravagant affair and as long as we agree that Gracie sticks close to you and me, then it should be fine."

"Gracie will be pleased." She took a drink and he thought about kissing her lips and tasting the bite of gin, the tang of lime that he knew would linger there.

An uncomfortable silence ensued and he fought the impulse to make an apology. He battled with his desire to get things between them the way they had been before the angry exchange of words.

He missed their closeness, missed the smiles she'd directed at him. He missed the comfortable silences they'd shared before, and dammit, he missed having her in his arms.

She set her glass on the coffee table and leaned back against the sofa cushion. "You said the other night that you'd stay until the filming wrapped up, then I should hire somebody else." She averted her gaze from his and instead focused on some point just beyond his shoulder. "Would you consider changing your mind and staying on until the danger is over?"

He wanted to say yes. Dear God, but he wanted to say yes, that he wouldn't abandon her or Gracie while any threats remained. But he knew that staying would be a mistake. Already it was going to be difficult enough telling her goodbye, telling Gracie goodbye. Spending more time with them would only make a bad situation worse.

Besides, he couldn't guarantee that if he continued to spend time here they wouldn't tumble into bed again. Even though they had fought, their angry words had done nothing to diminish the electricity that existed between them. Their confrontation had done nothing to douse the flames of desire that licked in his veins.

"I really don't think that's a good idea," he said with more than a touch of reluctance.

Her gaze returned to him and for a moment in the depth of her eyes he saw the whisper of longing, the hint of a vulnerability that arrowed through to his heart.

But even as he noted this, she stiffened her back and raised her chin. "I'm sure you're right. It will just be difficult getting Gracie to trust somebody as much as she trusts you."

"Gracie has a trusting soul. You shouldn't have too many problems. I'll help you find somebody that's good, somebody that you can trust with her safety."

"I'd appreciate it." She sat up and stroked a hand through her hair, the blond strands rippling with the action. "I guess we'd better call it a night. The party starts at noon tomorrow and now that Gracie is feeling so much better she'll be up and excited at the crack of dawn."

"I think I'll stay down here just a little bit longer," he said. The last thing he wanted to do was to follow her up the stairs, watch the sway of her hips as she made her way to the bedroom where they had made love.

She stood, once again her gaze not meeting his. "Then I guess I'll just see you in the morning."

"Good night, Libby."

"Good night." She carried her glass to the sink in the bar, then left the room, the familiar scent of her lingering long after she had gone.

Clay finished the last of his drink, then carried his glass to the sink. He rinsed both glasses, then moved to the window to stare out into the Hollywood night.

He had the urge to open the French doors and take a walk. He'd been cooped up all week helping Libby entertain Gracie. He felt the need to get outside, to feel the wind on his face and to breathe in the air untainted by Libby's perfume.

But he didn't go outside. Instead he leaned his forehead against the windowpane and watched the tops of the palm trees sway in the faint illumination from the ground lighting.

He could never live here. This place wasn't for him. His very soul was bound to the place he called home, a small town in Oklahoma where people didn't understand ulterior motives or machinations. He missed the red earth of Oklahoma, the deep, sweet grass and skies untainted by smog.

Maybe this kind of lifestyle was fine for some people, people like Libby who were driven by inner demons or blind ambitions. Maybe some people found happiness here, but he wasn't one of those people.

He turned away from the window with a sigh of frustration. There was a part of him that wanted to stay and see this job through. But there was another part of him that knew he had to leave.

Libby had asked him if he'd ever felt passionate about anything or anyone in his life and he'd replied that he had not. What he feared more than anything was that if he stayed here too long, if he allowed it to happen, he'd end up feeling passionate about loving Libby.

Libby awakened later than usual the next morning and she lingered in between the sheets, reluctant to get up and face another day.

When had that happened? When had her life become so difficult she was reluctant to face a new day? But even as she asked herself this, the answer was there in her mind. Her life had become difficult since the fight with Clay.

She missed the relationship they'd been building before they'd had that exchange of words, before he'd let her know what he really thought about her.

She tried to tell herself she didn't care what he thought. After all, he was just a bodyguard from a dusty little town. As much as she wanted to dismiss him as just that, she couldn't because he was so much more.

He was an intelligent, compassionate man who had the enviable position of being comfortable in his own skin, who never doubted his worth. And for just a few minutes after they had made love, Libby had felt the ugly whispering of doubts from her past quieted and she'd known a peace she'd never known before.

She'd known better than to get involved with him and

yet she'd done so anyway. Now she had to deal with the consequences. While she didn't wish away those moments in his arms, she wished the thought of him leaving didn't hurt quite so much.

Glancing at the clock on the nightstand she realized she needed to get up. It was going to be a busy day with the birthday party at noon.

It took her only a half an hour to shower and dress for the morning. She pulled on a pair of slacks and a blouse but would change into something cooler for the outdoor party.

She'd just left her bedroom when Gracie came racing down the hallway toward her, her little face wreathed in a smile. "Mr. Clay said we're going to Kathryn's birthday party," she exclaimed.

"Indeed, we are," Libby agreed. When Libby had been Gracie's age she hadn't been allowed to go to birthday parties or other social gatherings with children her own age. Her parents had proclaimed parties frivolous wastes of time. Nor had she ever had a birthday party of her own until she'd moved here and thrown herself a party two months ago when she'd turned twenty-six.

"It's going to be such fun," Gracie said as the two of them walked down the stairs. "There's going to be ponies, and I already told Mr. Clay he better not do to me what he did the last time when I was on a horse." She raised her little chin a notch and looked at her mother. "That wasn't nice."

"Mr. Clay apologized to you," Libby reminded her daughter.

Gracie nodded. "And he got boo-boos on his elbows."

They hit the bottom step and the scent of fresh-brewed coffee and fried bacon filled the air. "Hmmm, I smell breakfast," Libby said. "Why don't you go get settled in the dining room and I'll tell Helen we're ready to be served."

"What about Mr. Clay? We can't eat without him," Gracie protested.

"I'll go find him and tell him breakfast is ready," Libby replied. As she headed for the kitchen, she worried about how difficult it was going to be for Gracie when Clay said goodbye to them. Her daughter's heart would be broken. Unfortunately, it probably wouldn't be the last time Gracie's heart got broken.

She found Clay seated at the island in the kitchen. He had a cup of coffee in front of him and was staring out the window as Helen bustled to finish the last of the breakfast preparations.

For a long moment Libby did nothing to call attention to her presence, but instead simply stood and looked at Clay. Once again he was clad in jeans and a white, short-sleeved shirt that exposed taut biceps and tanned forearms.

A deep ache pierced through her as she remembered how good it had felt to be in his arms, how perfectly they had moved together as they had made love.

Her thoughts disturbed her and she briskly moved forward into the room. "Good morning."

Clay turned his head to look at her. "Good morning," he replied, no smile curving his lips or lighting the darkness of his eyes.

Libby missed his smiles. For the past week she'd seen few of them and most of the ones he'd displayed had been for Gracie, not for her.

"Breakfast is almost ready," Helen said as she pulled a tray of sliced fruit from the refrigerator.

"We're ready whenever you are," Libby said, then turned and left the kitchen. She had just seated herself in her chair at the table when Clay came in.

"Hey, munchkin." He ruffled the top of Gracie's head as he walked by her chair. "How's that ankle doing?"

"Good. It doesn't hurt at all anymore."

"That's excellent," Clay said as he sat at the table.

"Do you like clowns, Mr. Clay? Kathryn told me there's going to be lots of clowns at the birthday party."

Clay smiled at Gracie and Libby felt the warmth of his smile in the very pit of her stomach. "I love clowns," he said.

At that moment Helen came in to serve their meal. Thankfully Gracie chattered as they ate, easing the tension that had existed between Libby and Clay for the past week.

They had just finished eating when Helen returned to the dining room, a newspaper clutched in her hand. "I figured I'd let you eat in peace before letting you see this," she said to Libby.

Libby saw that the paper was one of the tabloids, a slightly sleazy one called the *Grapevine*. On the front page was a publicity shot of Gracie and the headline screamed, Death Threats Haunt America's Girl. Story On Page 10.

Two articles in two tabloids in less than a week, she thought in dismay.

"Mommy, look, it's me!" Gracie said as she saw the photo.

"Indeed, it is." Libby exchanged a quick glance with Clay, then looked back at Gracie. "Why don't you go find Molly and see if she'll help you wrap your present for the party."

Gracie looked at Clay. "We got Kathryn a Fashion Girl doll. It has real designer clothes and real diamond jewelry! She's gonna love it. I'll go find Molly and we'll wrap it so pretty."

As she whirled out of the dining room, Libby thumbed to page ten to read the article. Her fingers tightened as she read the words that told not only of Gracie's fall, but also of the letters she had received.

Without a word, she finished, then passed the paper to Clay. She watched him as he read. His jaw grew taut and when he was done he laid the paper on the table next to his plate and met her gaze.

"Do you know the reporter? Steve Stuttefield?"

"Never met him, never spoke to him and I can't imagine how he got the information that he printed," she replied.

Clay's eyes were dark and troubled. "The details of Gracie's fall had already been reported, but I'd like to know how this guy found out about the letters."

"I can count on three fingers the people who knew about them besides you and me. Charlie, the officer we initially went to about them, and the private investigator."

Clay frowned. "I suppose it's possible one of them sold the information to the reporter."

"I can't imagine any of them doing that," she replied.

"Well, if one of them didn't give out the information, then there's only one other person who could have." His gaze held hers intently.

"The person who wrote them." The words whispered from her.

Clay looked at his watch. "I'm going to try to get hold of this reporter this morning before we have to leave for the party. If I don't do it before, then when we get home I'll keep trying. I think we need to find out the source of his information."

"I thought reporters didn't have to give up their sources," Libby said.

His eyes narrowed and for the first time since she'd known him he looked dangerous. "Trust me, he'll give up his source to me."

Chapter 12

Clay should have known that a simple birthday party by Hollywood standards wasn't simple by anyone else's. When their car turned down the street where the Walker residence stood, several vans advertising the Clown Company and horse trailers were parked along the road. Interspersed among these were cars.

Gracie bounced with excitement between Clay and Libby, counting the horse trailers with glee. "Five! There's five," she exclaimed. "That means there's going to be five ponies to ride."

Clay looked at Libby and fought the usual burst of desire that swept through him. She looked as pretty as he'd ever seen her. The turquoise sundress hugged her slender curves, emphasized the thrust of her full breasts and did amazing things to the color of her eyes. The short dress exposed the length of her shapely legs and turquoise beaded sandals completed her look. Her hair was pulled back and clasped at the nape of her neck, highlighting her features.

Gracie was also clad in turquoise shorts and blouse, looking like a miniature of her gorgeous mother. In a million years Clay would have never imagined that two ladies could work their way so firmly into his heart. But at the moment he didn't have time to contemplate how that had happened. Instead he needed to focus on his surroundings.

He was pleased to discover that, like Libby's place, a high security wall surrounded the Walker residence. The only way in was through an electronic gate across the driveway.

As the gate opened to allow them entry, he was dismayed at the number of cars parked not only on the circular driveway, but also in a grassy area near the house.

"Are you all right?" Libby asked as the car came to a halt.

"Yeah, it just looks like there's going to be more people than I expected," he replied. More people meant more potential for trouble.

"Gracie, it's very important that while we're at the party, you stay close to either Mr. Clay or me, okay?" Libby eyed her daughter sternly.

"Okay, but I can ride a pony, right?"

Libby smiled. "Yes, you can ride a pony."

Together the three of them got out of the car and headed for the front door. Clay walked just behind Libby and

Gracie and tried to keep his gaze away from the alluring sway of Libby's bottom.

Richard greeted them at the door and welcomed them in with a slightly strained smile. "Welcome to chaos," he said. "I never knew a birthday party could be so noisy."

"Looks like you have a crowd here," Clay said as they followed Richard through his house and to a back door.

"I think there are more clowns and ponies than kids at this point, but I'm not sure. I think I've lost count," he replied. He'd just opened the back door when the doorbell rang. "Please, go enjoy."

As he hurried back toward the front door, Clay followed Gracie and Libby into the backyard. Clay's breath caught in his throat as he surveyed what had once been a normal backyard and now looked like a three-ring circus.

A huge inflated moonwalk took up one corner of the yard and at the opposite end of the yard a half dozen ponies were already burdened with squirming, squealing children riding their backs.

Clowns wandered in the crowd, twisting balloons into animals, blowing bubbles and doing pratfalls to the delight of their young audience.

Clay stood next to Libby, a restraining hand on Gracie's shoulder as he assessed the situation. So many people, both adults and children, he thought.

"Gracie!" The red-haired Kathryn screamed and waved from the back of one of the ponies.

Gracie looked up at Clay. "Can I go ride a pony with Kathryn?"

"We'll all go," he said. As Gracie ran ahead, he and Libby hurried to keep up.

"Most of these kids and their parents we've known for some time," Libby said from beside him. "Other than the people working the party, I don't see anyone that I wouldn't trust."

Clay frowned and once again swept the area with a discerning gaze. It was difficult to imagine danger raising its head here, amid the brightly colored balloons and laughing children. And yet he knew danger had no conscience when it came to where it raised its head.

He looked back at Libby. "We're probably safe here, but I still want to keep an eye on her and not allow her to get too far from either you or me." He offered her a smile. "In the meantime, I think maybe the best thing to do is relax and enjoy this circus."

She returned his smile, as if grateful for his words of reassurance. "It is a circus, isn't it?"

Clay watched as Gracie was helped onto the back of a pony and he and Libby waved as she waved at them. "Is this the kind of party Gracie gets on her birthdays?"

"She's never had ponies or moonwalks before. I'm just hoping this doesn't set some sort of precedent in her mind. I pay my gardeners too much to let ponies run amuck in my backyard."

"Whatever happened to a handful of friends and a birthday cake being enough?"

"I don't know. I never even had that much when I was

growing up." There was no self-pity in her words. They were merely a statement of fact.

"No birthday parties for Libby?" he asked. What kind of parents had raised her?

"Birthdays are nothing special. It's just another day and chores need to get done same as any other day, that's what my parents used to tell me." She smiled at him and shrugged, a hardness shining from her eyes. "I imagine if Gracie wants ponies on her next birthday, we'll have ponies and damn the gardens."

Clay laughed, for the moment enjoying the conversation without the tension that had marked their relationship for the past week. He wanted it to continue, the easiness, the camaraderie. "Birthdays were big deals in our house when I was growing up."

Her bright blue eyes gazed at him with interest. "I'll bet that cook of yours baked your favorite cake and all your brothers and sister got you presents."

"Not only that, but the birthday person always got to pick what we'd eat for supper that night. I was always pretty boring. I'd want hot dogs and fries. Meredith always wanted cinnamon rolls and steak. Joshua was a spaghetti and pineapple salad kind of kid." He stopped, realizing he was about to chronicle every birthday meal for everyone in his family. "Sorry, I was about to bore you silly."

"On the contrary, I like hearing about your family." She sighed wistfully. "I wish I had similar stories to share."

Their attention was torn from each other as Gracie

called to them. She pointed to the moonwalk and took off running toward the big colorful structure.

"I have a feeling this is going to be the extent of our time here, running after Gracie," Libby said as they hurried toward the moonwalk.

Clay smiled and watched as Gracie got into the air-filled enclosure and began bouncing around with half a dozen other children.

"Yoo-hoo," a familiar voice hollered from nearby. Clay turned to see Delores Gleason hurrying toward them, a bright smile wreathing her plump face. He heard Libby's sigh just before Delores descended upon them.

"Darlings, it's so good to see you here," she said. "I was wondering how little Gracie had healed from her trauma on the set."

"She's just fine," Libby said.

"It's always lovely when the children can get together for a little bit of fun. These children, they're so special. It's important we keep them as well-adjusted as possible. I was just telling Malcolm the other day that…"

Clay zoned out as she talked and talked and talked, reminding them of her son's talent, how they were just waiting for the perfect vehicle to make him a real star and how hard she was preparing him to be the next top dog in G-rated movies.

Thankfully, Malcolm chose that moment to ride a pony and the instant the pony took its first step Malcolm screamed for his mother.

"Oh dear, please excuse me. Malcolm is such a sensitive child." She scurried in the direction of the ponies.

"Poor Malcolm, dealing with Delores, he'll probably be an alcoholic before he's ten," Libby said.

"If she would have talked to us for another couple of minutes I might have taken up drinking," Clay said dryly, and was rewarded by Libby's laugh.

A few minutes later as Gracie sat with a bunch of other children watching two clowns perform, Libby and Clay sat on folding chairs just behind the group.

It wasn't just the sound of Libby's laughter that he liked to hear. Gracie's laughter touched him, brought a smile to his lips.

He turned to look at Libby, noting how the sun sparked in her hair, how her dress complemented her complexion, her eyes. "You know, I told you on the night of the movie premiere that red was your color, but I was wrong," he said. "Turquoise is definitely your color. You look pretty today."

Her cheeks pinkened and she held his gaze for a long moment. "Gracie is going to miss you when you're gone."

"Kids are resilient. She'll be fine."

"What about me?" She looked down at the ground, her long lashes shading her cheeks. "How am I going to be when you leave?"

He wasn't sure what to say, was surprised to realize emotion once again pressed tight in his chest. "You'll be just like you were before I got here," he said. "You'll be strong and focused and independent."

She raised her gaze to meet his. "I never expected this. I thought I could sleep with you and not care about you." She emitted a small laugh. "I guess I'm less Hollywood than I thought I was."

"You make that sound like a bad thing," he said teasingly, needing to keep it light. But it was impossible to keep it light where she was concerned. "I care about you, too, Libby, but this isn't some Hollywood movie with a built-in happy ending."

She sighed, a deep sigh that was filled with longing and regret. "I know. I just wish—"

Whatever she'd been about to say was cut off by a child's scream that rent the air.

Libby jumped to her feet, her heart crashing against her ribs as her gaze sought Gracie. She instantly relaxed when she realized Gracie still sat in the group of children watching the clowns.

The scream had come from Malcolm, who was apparently in the throes of a full-blown temper tantrum. As Delores did her best to calm her son, Richard announced from the back deck that hamburgers and hot dogs were being served.

Minutes later Libby and Clay sat with Gracie between them at one of the picnic tables. "There's five clowns," Gracie said between bites of a hot dog. "There's Bonzo, he's the one with the funny hat, and Smiley with the white smile, and Coco who makes the balloon animals."

She paused to take another bite, then continued. "Then there's Crackers who falls all the time and Bubbles."

"Who blows bubbles," Libby interjected.

"That's right." Gracie beamed at her mother, then sighed dramatically. "I love clowns."

"And you love ponies," Clay said.

Gracie nodded. "I love clowns and ponies and Mommy and you."

Libby saw the effect of Gracie's words on Clay. She saw the stab of pain that darkened his green eyes, the deep swallow that knotted his throat.

"I love you, too, munchkin," he said, his voice deeper than usual. "And now, you'd better eat the rest of that hot dog before I eat it for you."

Gracie giggled and quickly picked up the hot dog. It was at that moment that Libby realized neither she nor Gracie would ever be quite the same when Clay left their lives.

His presence had done more than keep Gracie safe. He'd shown them what it might be like to have a male in their house, in their lives, in their hearts.

She was in love with him. The realization ripped through her like a lightning bolt rent the clouds. For the first time in her life, she was in love and there was no happy ending in sight.

The laughter surrounding her echoed hollowly in her ears and the bright colors of party balloons and streamers faded beneath the aching pain that settled in the pit of her stomach.

She was in love with Clay West and in a week he'd be gone from her life. She'd long ago become accustomed to the well of loneliness that had been with her all her life, but she had a feeling when Clay left that well would be deeper and more painful than ever.

She straightened her back and bit into her hamburger. And she would survive. Because that's what she did. She and Gracie would be fine. They had her work, their social events. They didn't need a cowboy to make them complete.

After lunch there was cake and ice cream, then it came time for Kathryn to open the mound of presents.

Gracie sat with friends on the lawn while Libby and Clay sat nearby on chairs with some of the other parents.

"I'll be right back," Clay said, and gestured toward the house. "I'm going to try to call that reporter again and it's too noisy out here."

She nodded and watched as he walked away, pulling his cell phone from his pocket. She didn't let her gaze linger on his broad back, but instead returned her attention to Kathryn and the unwrapping of the gifts.

Delores slid into the seat Clay had vacated, a glass of white wine in her hand. It was obvious that it wasn't her first, or probably her fourth glass of wine.

Her eyes had the glazed expression of a woman who had overimbibed. "That man is some hunk." The words slurred out of her. "Honey, you'd better not let him out of your sight." She leaned closer to Libby and her wineglass bumped her knee, tossing the contents onto Libby's skirt.

"Oh, dear, I'm so sorry. Here, let me help you." Delores took her napkin and swiped at Libby's skirt. "I can't believe I did that."

"It's all right." Libby used her own napkin and dabbed at the wet spot. "At least it was white wine instead of red."

"I'm just so sorry. I'll pay for the dry cleaning," Delores said, obviously distraught.

"Really, Delores, it's fine. In this heat it will be dry in no time and besides it's not dry-cleaning material." Libby finished dabbing at the area, then settled back in her chair once again.

"I'm just going to refill my glass," Delores said, and rose a bit unsteadily to her feet.

Libby nodded absently and her gaze went toward the group of children. Where Gracie had sat only moments before was now an empty space.

She looked over to the ponies, wondering if Gracie had decided to have another ride. But there was no sign of her blond-haired child in her bright blue shorts set.

Libby's heart began an unsteady beat. Don't panic, she told herself as she stood, her gaze shooting to the left, then to the right. There was no sign of Gracie anywhere.

Don't panic, she told herself once again. Maybe she was inside the moonwalk. Libby broke into a run toward the inflated play enclosure. As she got closer she could hear the sounds of kids laughing and playing inside.

Be there, Gracie, she begged. She ran to the entry and peered inside. Her heart exploded into full-blown fear as she saw that Gracie wasn't inside.

Half-blind with her fear, she raced back toward the house. In the bathroom. Maybe she'd had to use the bathroom and had run inside the house.

She collided with Clay in the back doorway. "Whoa." He grabbed her by the shoulders, but when he got a look at her face he tensed.

"I can't find Gracie," she said, and swallowed against the tears that threatened to erupt. "Please help me. I can't find her. I can't find her anywhere."

Chapter 13

Clay's blood went cold. He tightened his grip on Libby's shoulders as he saw the frantic fear in her eyes, heard the rising hysteria in her voice. "Calm down and tell me what's going on."

She took a deep breath and he felt the trembling of her body beneath his fingertips. "Delores spilled some wine on me. I was cleaning myself up and I was distracted and when I finished and looked over to where Gracie had been sitting she was gone."

Clay tried not to panic as he gazed over Libby's shoulder at the crowd in the backyard. It would be easy to lose sight of a child in the crush of little people. "Don't get excited. I'm sure she's around here someplace. Did you check the moonwalk?" he asked as he released her.

"She's not there. I checked. I checked the moonwalk and the ponies." She reached out and wrapped her hand around his forearm, squeezing painfully hard. "She's not anywhere."

Clay pulled away from her grip and headed into the yard, his gaze shooting frantically around in search of Gracie. He swallowed against the rising panic as he didn't see her anywhere.

She had to be here. They were just missing her. Where else could she be?

"Kathryn, have you seen Gracie?" he called to the little girl still unwrapping presents. "Anyone seen Gracie?" There must have been something in his voice that alerted the adults in the group that something was wrong.

"She was sitting over there a little while ago," Delores said, and pointed to a group of children seated in the grass.

Richard came striding over to Clay. "Is something wrong?"

· "We can't find Gracie," Clay said tersely. Dammit, he should have never left to make that phone call.

Richard frowned in confusion. "What do you mean?"

"I mean, we can't find her. She doesn't appear to be here."

"Is she in the house? Maybe she went to the bathroom or is playing in Kathryn's room," Richard suggested.

Of course. A rush of relief swept through him. Kathryn was Gracie's best friend. It was possible Gracie had gotten bored with the party and had gone inside to play with some of Kathryn's toys.

Clay turned on his heels and headed back to the house, aware of Richard following behind him. "We need to check the house," Clay told Libby, who stood white-faced, eyes huge, on the back deck.

"But you were inside," Libby said. "Did you see her come in?"

"I was in the dining room making some calls. I wasn't paying any attention to people coming and going." Dammit. Guilt ripped through him. He should have never left the backyard. He should have never taken his eyes off Gracie. It was his job to watch over her.

"Gracie!" Libby cried as they entered the house. "Gracie, are you in here?"

"Kathryn's room is up the stairs, the second room on the left," Richard said.

Clay took the stairs two at a time and tried to ignore the overwhelming sense of dread that made his legs feel unusually heavy, caused his heart to pound as if it might explode from his chest.

Kathryn's room was pretty, decorated in bright yellows and white. It had the requisite ruffles and bows, dolls and toys. What it didn't have was Gracie.

It was at that moment that cold, stark fear filled Clay's soul. Gracie was no place in the backyard or in the house. Gracie was gone.

He flew back down the stairs where Richard and Libby stood. "I'm calling the police," he said to Richard.

"Oh, God." Libby reeled backward and would have fallen if Richard hadn't grabbed her.

"I don't understand. Could she have wandered off the property?" Richard asked. "Maybe we should check the streets. You know how kids are, sometimes they just don't think."

Libby shook her head. "She would have never wandered off." Tears ran down her cheeks as she stepped away from Richard and toward Clay.

Clay withdrew his cell phone and quickly punched in a number. "Detective Holt, Clay West. We're at the residence of Richard Walker at a birthday party and Gracie has disappeared from the party." He quickly gave the detective Richard's address, then clicked off.

"What happens now?" Libby asked, and leaned into Clay, as if her legs threatened to buckle once again.

"We wait for the police." He tightened an arm around her and looked at Richard. "Nobody comes in and nobody leaves this house until the police arrive."

"Of course," Richard replied. "In the meantime I'll get some of the adults to look again around the backyard. Maybe she's there and you both just missed seeing her."

As he headed for the back door, Libby fell apart. "It's all my fault." Deep, wrenching sobs tore through her as she buried her face in the front of his shirt. "I took my eyes off her." Her voice rose an octave and Clay suspected she was one sob away from hysteria. "I got distracted. If anything happens to her I'll never forgive myself."

"Libby." He took her by the shoulders and held her at arm's length. "Look at me," he said forcefully. Her eyes were pools of torture as she met his gaze. "You need to be strong. If anyone is to blame for this it's me, not you. Guarding Gracie was my job and I screwed up." His voice choked from him as a wealth of emotion crawled up his throat.

"No, no, I don't blame you," she replied, and wiped at her tears. "I just…I just don't know who to blame and I'm so scared."

"We'll find her. I swear, it's going to be all right." Even as he said the words he prayed that they were true. But an icy chill filled him as he realized they had no clues, no leads, nothing to tell them who might have taken Gracie and what the person intended to do with her.

Within fifteen minutes Detective Holt arrived, flanked by a handful of uniformed cops. He interviewed both Clay and Libby, who seemed to be holding together by a mere thread, as his cops canvassed the area.

The party had taken on a somber air as everyone was asked questions and Holt got an invitation list from Richard. He checked the list against the people who were present, trying to figure out who might have disappeared from the party at the same time that Gracie had.

Minutes passed in agonizing increments. Libby remained next to Clay, her features radiating the hollowness of a shell-shocked victim.

He wanted to assure her. He wanted to take her in his arms and tell her that Gracie would be okay, but he couldn't. His heart ached with a fear that was nearly consuming. He was filled with an impotent rage that had no focus.

He'd failed. He'd failed Libby, but most of all he'd failed Gracie. The thought of his little girl being frightened, being hurt…or worse, pierced his soul with a pain he'd carry with him forever.

The children seemed unaware of the drama playing out. They continued to play, to laugh and wrestle with each other. Their laughter rang in his ears, increasing his pain as what he wanted to hear more than anything was Gracie's sweet laughter.

The most frustrating part of all was that he wanted to bust somebody's head open. He needed to tear somebody up, but had no idea who to go after.

He released his hold on Libby and strode over to Detective Holt, who was interviewing Delores Gleason. Delores, who had spilled the drink on Libby, providing the distraction that had allowed Gracie to disappear.

As he walked toward the woman the rage that he'd kept in check threatened to explode. But as she gazed at him, her eyes blurred with drink, her makeup smeared down her cheeks from tears, he checked himself. Delores was too stupid to engineer a kidnapping. Besides, she had no motive that he could imagine.

He tapped Holt's sleeve. The detective whirled around to face him. "I just thought of something," Clay said. "I've been trying to get hold of a reporter who wrote a story that appeared this morning in the *Grapevine*. His name is Steve Stuttefield and he wrote about the letters Gracie had received. That information hadn't been made public. I want to know his source."

Holt wrote the information on a piece of paper, then motioned one of the uniformed officers to him. "Find this guy and get him to tell his source for a story that appeared this morning in his rag sheet," he instructed the officer who nodded and took off in the direction of the house.

As Clay walked back to where Libby stood on the deck, he scanned the crowd once again. He frowned as his brain made a connection it hadn't before.

He hurried toward Libby. "When Gracie was sitting with us to eat she mentioned there were five clowns. There was the one who made balloon animals, the one with the funny hat." He frowned again as he tried to remember what Gracie had said.

"Crackers, the one who falls down, and Smiley with the white smile." Libby looked around, then her eyes widened and she stared at Clay. "Bubbles. Bubbles is missing, too."

Cold. Libby had never been so cold in her life. The chill didn't just whisper across her skin, but rather invaded deep into her bones, deep into her very soul.

She watched as Clay called information to get the number for the Clown Company. Where was Gracie? Where in God's name was her daughter?

If Bubbles the Clown had taken her, then why? What did he plan to do to her? She didn't allow her mind to travel down that particular road too far, for the possibilities were torturous.

"I've got to go," Clay said as he hung up his cell phone. "I've got an address." He headed out the front door.

"Wait, I'm coming with you," Libby cried, and ran after him.

He opened the driver's door of the limo and motioned a surprised Raymond out from behind the wheel. "You should stay here," he said to Libby.

"Like hell I will," she retorted, and yanked open the passenger door. She'd go mad if she just sat, waiting for something to happen. She needed to be doing something, going somewhere in search of her daughter.

"Things could get dangerous," he said as he started the engine with a roar.

"Yes, they could, for whoever took Gracie from me."

He handed her his cell phone as he squealed down the driveway toward the open gate. "Call Holt and tell him we're headed to 522 Mimosa Lane."

Libby delivered the message, then pulled the seat belt around her and fastened it as Clay sped down the street toward the highway.

"Why would a clown working a children's birthday party want to kidnap Gracie?" she asked, talking around the lump that had taken up residence in the back of her throat.

"I don't know, but I hope we have the answer in just a few minutes." His hands were so tight on the steering wheel his knuckles were white. "The Clown Company guy I spoke to on the phone told me that Bubbles's real name is Matthew Santori. Ever heard of him?"

Matthew Santori? She turned the name around and around in her head. "No, never."

She turned her head to stare unseeing out the passenger window. Please, please let her be okay. Please, don't let anything bad happen to my baby. Tears once again blurred her vision. She felt physically ill with the need to hold Gracie tight, to feel her little heartbeat against her own.

Five twenty-two Mimosa. Please, let Gracie be there. The scenery whirled by in a sea of frightened tears. Her heart beat so hard, so fast, she could scarcely breathe.

Clay pulled the car over to the curb. They were in a neighborhood of small bungalows. "Stay here," he commanded. She watched as he flipped the safety off his gun. "I don't know what I might be walking into. You stay here and wait for the police to arrive." With those words he left the car and headed up the sidewalk.

"Like hell," Libby said to herself. She'd never taken orders well from anyone and she wasn't about to start now. She didn't give a damn about her personal safety. All she wanted was to make sure Gracie was safe. She got out of the car and followed Clay.

He shot a glance backward and scowled as she hurried to catch up with him. "Don't you ever listen to anybody?" His voice was a low growl.

"Not when it comes to my daughter," she replied.

"For God's sake, stay behind me."

She did as he requested. The last thing she wanted to do was to get in his way or to create more problems, but she sure as hell wasn't going to sit in the car. She wanted the first face Gracie saw to be Clay's coming to her rescue, but the second face Gracie would need to see was Libby's.

Five twenty-two Mimosa was a white bungalow with bright blue trim. A small front porch held a wicker rocker with blue cushions and as they approached a fat white cat jumped off the rocker and disappeared under the porch. There was no car in the driveway and Libby fought an overwhelming sense of despair.

Clay walked up to the front door and banged on it with his fist. "Santori! Open up." It was obvious he intended wasting no time. Without waiting for a response, he reared back and hit the door with his shoulder with a force that splintered the door frame.

He shoved through the door, gun drawn. "Gracie! Are you in here?" Libby shouted as she followed Clay into an empty living room.

Clay moved to the kitchen. Also empty. Libby followed him out of the kitchen and that's when she heard it. A thud. Then another.

"Clay," she whispered, and pointed to the pantry closet door. "It's coming from there."

He grabbed her and shoved her behind him, then reached out for the pantry door. He jerked it open and a man tumbled to the floor in front of them.

Libby gasped and Clay cursed and shoved his gun into the waistband of his slacks. The man on the floor stared up at them with frightened brown eyes. His hands and feet were bound with rope and a strip of duct tape rode his mouth.

Clay leaned down and ripped the tape from his mouth. "Matthew Santori?"

The man nodded. "Thank God you found me. I thought I was going to die in there."

Libby stared at the man, then looked up at Clay. "If he's Bubbles the Clown, then who has Gracie? Oh, God, Clay, where's my baby?"

At that moment Holt arrived with his men. He scowled at Clay and Libby as he entered the kitchen. "You two running amuck makes me nervous." He gestured to the man on the floor. "What have we got here?"

"Meet the real Bubbles the Clown," Clay said, and Libby heard the wind of despair blowing in his voice.

It took fifteen minutes to find out what had happened. Matthew had been in the process of dressing for the Walker party when a man had burst through his front door with a gun.

The man had bound him, then proceeded to dress in the Bubbles costume and makeup. When he was dressed, he'd shoved Matthew into the pantry closet and left.

"What did he look like?" Holt asked.

Matthew, now seated on the sofa in the living room frowned. "Short, kind of beefy. Tanned with blond hair cut in a buzz."

Clay looked at Libby and she shook her head. The description didn't fit anyone she knew. But he had a gun. The man who had burst into this house and dressed himself like a clown to attend the party had a gun.

The man who had Gracie had a gun.

With each moment that passed the sickness in Libby's soul grew more pronounced and what scared her more than anything was that she saw the same soul sickness radiating from Clay's eyes.

Holt stopped to take a phone call and when he disconnected, he looked at Clay. "That was one of my men. He just picked up that reporter you wanted to talk to and is on his way here with him."

"Good." Clay's voice was cold.

Time. Time was passing. Time was wasting and they were no closer to knowing where Gracie was than they'd been the minute they'd discovered her gone.

The despair that Libby had been fighting threatened to engulf her, to cast her into a dark place where she might never return.

As if sensing the darkness of her thoughts, the depth of her emotions, Clay put an arm around her shoulder. "Maybe the reporter will have some information for us," he said softly.

She hoped so. She hoped Steve Stuttefield would be able to give them information that would lead to Gracie. And she hoped…prayed that it wouldn't be too late.

Steve Stuttefield was a small man with stooped shoulders and an unusually large nose that gave him the appearance of a rodent.

He was led into Bubbles's living room by a uniformed cop and it was obvious by the look on his face that he wasn't happy about being there.

"I'm under deadline and don't appreciate being pulled away from my desk by a cop with an attitude," he exclaimed, and glared at the officer who had accompanied him in.

If he thinks the cop has attitude, wait until I get through with him, Clay thought. With every moment that passed, the guilt and the rage inside Clay had grown. But neither of those emotions was as bad as the terror that clawed at his guts, that ripped at his heart as he thought of Gracie.

He should have never allowed them to go to the party. But he'd gotten too close, lost his objectivity. He hadn't wanted to disappoint the little girl who had professed her love for him. Dammit, he should have known better.

With all these emotions railing inside him, he dropped his arm from Libby's shoulder and approached Steve Stuttefield. "This morning an article appeared in your paper about Gracie Bryant."

"Yeah, so?" Despite the fact that he was a foot shorter than Clay, he raised his chin and looked at Clay with challenge.

"I want to know your source."

"Yeah and I'd like to write for *Newsweek*," he said dryly. "Get a life, buddy. I don't divulge my sources."

Clay snapped. He didn't plan to. It just happened. He grabbed Stuttefield by the front of his shirt and yanked him up so his rodent nose was inches in front of his own. Stuttefield squeaked a protest.

"You will divulge this source or I'll make sure you never write a story again in your life." Clay heard the deep menace in his own voice.

"Let me go," Stuttefield cried. "What the hell is your problem?"

"Right now you are my problem," Clay replied, fighting the red veil of rage that threatened to descend.

"Let him go, Mr. West," Holt said.

"Not until he tells me where he got his information," Clay replied, and meant it. He was at the point of busting heads to get what he wanted. Something had to break for them to get a handle on what had happened to Gracie, and if that something was Stuttefield's head, then that was fine by him.

Stuttefield must have seen the intent in Clay's eyes. "All right. All right, just let me go." Clay released him and he stumbled backward, glaring at Clay balefully. "I can't give you a name because I don't have one."

"How were you contacted?" Holt asked.

"A man called my cell phone two days ago and gave me the information. He told me about the fall at the studio, about some brick being thrown through her bedroom window and some letters she'd been getting, and that's all I know."

"But surely you got a number," Clay said, and narrowed his eyes. "A reporter like you would want to keep the number of a source."

"He didn't give me the number," he replied, but his gaze didn't meet Clay's.

"But you have caller ID on your cell phone. You've probably got his number stored." Bingo. Clay held out his hand. "Give me your phone."

Stuttefield hesitated, once again challenge gleaming from his eyes.

"I believe I'd do as he asks," Holt said. "If he attacks you again, I'm not sure my men will be able to pull him off before he seriously hurts you."

Stuttefield cursed softly beneath his breath, then pulled his cell phone from his pocket, punched a few buttons, then handed it to Clay. "There. That's it, the number of the man who called me."

Clay read the number out loud and looked at Libby. "Recognize it?"

She shook her head.

"Then let's find out who it belongs to." He punched in the numbers and held the phone to his ear. It rang once. Twice.

"Hello?"

It was a deep, familiar voice. Clay disconnected the call and stared at Libby. The bleakness in her eyes called to him, made him aware that it wasn't just Gracie's life on the line, but Libby's, as well. If anything bad happened to Gracie, he didn't know if Libby could survive.

"Walker. It was Richard Walker," he said.

Chapter 14

They were once again in the car, racing back to the Walker house and Libby was trying to make sense of everything. Why would Richard leak the story of the letters to the press? And more importantly how had he known about the letters?

"You're sure you didn't mention the letters to him," Clay asked, obviously sharing her brain waves.

"Positive. I told you before I didn't tell anyone except Charlie, the officer and the investigator about those letters. There's no way Richard could have known about them unless he wrote them." Her racing heart had not slowed since the moment she'd realized Gracie was gone.

It had now been more than two and a half hours since she'd first discovered Gracie missing. It was just after six o'clock. In another couple of hours night would come and

Libby couldn't imagine the night falling without Gracie in her arms.

She turned to look at Clay. Once again he held the steering wheel in a tight grasp and his features were set in stone. Over the past couple of hours she'd seen the rage that radiated from Clay's eyes. She'd seen his anger, but she'd also seen the guilt that tormented him.

She'd told him the truth. She didn't blame him for Gracie's disappearance. Just as she couldn't blame herself too much. They'd thought it was safe and even though they had tried to be vigilant, they had messed up. They'd messed up and now Gracie was gone.

He glanced her way and his strong features softened. "You've got to stay strong, Libby."

"I know." She drew a trembling breath. "I'm just so afraid. I've never been this afraid." She didn't feel strong. When she thought of Gracie being frightened, or worse, her heart threatened to stop beating altogether. "What I don't understand is why Richard would call the reporter about those letters. What did he expect to gain?"

"Who knows?" He shot her another glance. "But I have to tell you, just because we suspect Richard wrote those letters and contacted Stuttefield, it doesn't mean he has anything to do with Gracie's disappearance."

"Don't say that," she said with a touch of panic. "Because if Richard doesn't know something about all this, then we have nothing."

What frightened her as much as anything was that Clay didn't reply and his silence spoke louder than a scream in her head. Richard had to have some answers, otherwise she was terrified that all would be lost.

Before Clay had turned off the car's engine, Libby was out of the vehicle and racing toward the Walker front door. She was vaguely aware of Detective Holt's car pulling up behind theirs.

She was just about to go through the door when Clay grabbed her arm and turned her around to face him. "No matter what happens in there, we'll find her."

She wanted to believe him, desperately needed to believe him, but she knew the truth of the matter. If Richard Walker wasn't involved in any of this, then they had nothing to go on, no leads whatsoever.

The police were still at the house and the party was still in full swing in the backyard. Together, Detective Holt, Libby and Clay walked outside to find Richard.

The moment Libby saw the man standing near the ponies, a cold, hard knot formed in her chest. At the worst, he knew something about Gracie's kidnapping. At the very least he had gone out of his way to provide information to a reporter in an attempt to hurt Gracie's career.

He smiled hesitantly as he watched her approach. "Did you find her?"

A buzzing began in Libby's head. All conscious thought unraveled as she stepped up to him and slapped him across the face. The blow was delivered with such force she felt it all the way up into her shoulder.

He roared in outrage and raised a fist. Clay stepped

between him and Libby. "Touch her and I'll kill you," Clay said with soft menace.

His cheek flame-red, Richard glared at her. "What the hell is wrong with you?" He reached up and rubbed his cheek. "Have you gone absolutely mad?"

"That was for the story that appeared in this morning's edition of the *Grapevine*," Libby said. "You bastard." The words ripped from her throat. "What have you done with my daughter?"

"She's crazy!" Richard looked at Clay, at Holt, then back at her. "Libby, you're distraught. I don't know what you're talking about and I didn't do anything with Gracie."

She wanted to scratch his eyes out, slap his other cheek. She needed to scream at somebody, to rail until somebody told her where Gracie was.

He looked at Holt. "Detective, this is insane. I've been here all afternoon. Any of these people can tell you that."

She'd thought she'd cried every bit of moisture out of her body, but tears once again spilled down her face and she watched as Clay pulled his cell phone from his pocket.

"We talked to Stuttefield. He gave us the number of the man who called him and told him about the letters Gracie had received." Clay's voice held a cold calm that under other circumstances would have frightened her. She held her breath as he punched in the numbers.

A cell phone rang in response. Richard's cell phone. The other side of his face turned as brilliant red as the side Libby had slapped.

"Okay," he exclaimed. "So I called that reporter. That doesn't mean anything."

"You bastard," Libby repeated. "Where's my daughter?"

"I don't know! I admit I called Stuttefield, but I don't know anything about what happened to Gracie," Richard exclaimed.

"Let me have your cell phone." Clay's voice was still deadly calm. But Libby smelled the approach of a storm and she welcomed it. She wanted him to rip Richard's head off, hit him until he told them what they wanted to hear.

"Go to hell," Richard replied, and took a step back from Clay. "I don't have to do anything you say."

Clay's eyes narrowed. "We can do this the easy way or we can do it the hard way. It doesn't matter to me, but one way or another I'm going to have your cell phone."

"Aren't you going to stop this?" Richard demanded of Holt.

The detective shrugged his thick shoulders. "I'd be interested in seeing your cell phone, too."

"I want an attorney." Richard's attractive features twisted into a mask of indignation.

Clay took a step toward him. "A dead man doesn't need an attorney."

Tension rippled in the air as Clay and Richard faced off. Libby bit back a scream of frustration, then nearly sobbed in relief as Richard held out his phone.

Clay punched a couple of buttons, then threw the phone to the ground. "Hollywood Night Motel." He glared at Richard. "You want to tell me why a call came into you from the Hollywood Night Motel twenty minutes after Gracie disappeared from the party?"

"Wrong number," Richard said, but his features radiated guilt.

"Take him into custody." Holt gestured to Walker and as an officer moved forward to do as he bid, Holt and his partner turned and headed toward the house.

Hollywood Night Motel. Hollywood Night Motel. The words repeated themselves in Libby's head as she and Clay followed Holt. Let Gracie be there and please, please let her be alive.

"We're going with you," Clay said as they all reached Holt's car.

Holt frowned. "We don't even know for sure she's there. We're just playing a hunch."

"Please," Libby said to the rumpled, overweight man. "Please, she'll need me."

His frown softened slightly and he pointed to the back seat. "Get in, but once we get to the motel I want both of you to stay in the car and out of our way."

Moments later they sped down the street and Libby tried to keep her horror at bay. Without Gracie there was nothing. She couldn't imagine her life without Gracie in it.

The tears that had plagued her off and on throughout the ordeal once again burned hot in her eyes. She reached out for Clay's hand, grateful when his fingers curled around hers.

There was strength in his hand, strength in his gaze, and

she realized for the first time in her life that she was bereft of strength.

"That call came into Walker's phone about twenty minutes after Gracie disappeared," Clay said to the detective. "I figure it was a check-in to let Walker know he was there with Gracie."

Holt nodded, then made several radio calls, his brief conversation peppered with numbers and codes Libby didn't understand.

"We can't go in like the cavalry," Holt said as he continued to exceed the speed limit. "We know the perp has a gun and we don't know what he's capable of."

Although he was speaking to his partner, Libby had the feeling his words were specifically intended for her and Clay. She wanted the cavalry. She wanted a SWAT team, the air force and the U.S. Marines there to get her baby back in her arms.

Gracie was all she had, all she'd ever had. The idea of having to endure day after day of life without Gracie was too horrible to imagine.

When they reached the motel, Holt parked at one end of the parking lot. "I'll go into the office and see what they can tell me about anyone who has checked in during the afternoon."

"That's not necessary," Clay said as he released Libby's hand. He pointed to a red SUV parked in front of Unit 110. "That SUV was at Walker's earlier today."

Holt half turned in his seat with a frown. "Are you sure?"

"Positive. I remember the sticker on the back bumper."

Libby looked at the SUV and noticed the sticker that read I Love My German Shepherd. She stared at the unit where the curtains were pulled shut.

Was Gracie inside or had something terrible already happened and her body had been cast to the side of a lonely road? She swallowed the sob that thought evoked.

"We need to get a look inside." Holt turned back around to stare at the unit. "I'm reluctant to break down the door and go in without knowing what's on the other side."

"It's going to be hard to get a look inside with the curtains drawn tight," his partner, Detective Mitchell observed.

Holt frowned. "It would be better if we could get him to open the door for us."

Libby gazed around frantically. What were they going to do? Now that she was here and there was the possibility that Gracie was so near, she sure as hell didn't want to sit patiently while the police tried to figure out what to do. Time was wasting.

"We should wait for the SWAT team," Holt said.

Wait? She couldn't wait. She needed them to do something now. "No, no. I have an idea," Libby said. She frowned, wondering if she could pull it off. Somehow she had to get him to open the door for her, she had to get a look inside to see if she saw any sign of Gracie.

She looked at Holt. "I can get him to open the door. Just get me a pair of pants."

He looked at her blankly. "Pants?"

"Any kind of slacks." She pulled her hair from the

barrette at the nape of her neck and shook it free as Holt disappeared from the car. He went to the trunk of the car and opened it.

"What are you doing, Libby?" Clay asked.

"I'm going to get him to open that door."

"But he probably saw you at the party. He'll recognize you as Gracie's mom," Clay protested.

"No, he won't." She used her hands to tousle her hair wildly around her head, then scrubbed at her eyes with the backs of her hands, smearing her eye makeup beneath her eyes. "What he saw at the birthday party was Libby Byrant, Hollywood mother. What he's going to see at the door of that motel room is somebody quite different."

Holt got back into the car with a pair of sweatpants in hand. "You want to tell me what you intend to do with these?"

Libby took them from him and pulled them on, then pulled her sundress over her head, leaving her clad in a lacy white camisole.

"Libby!" Clay protested.

She glared at him. "Look around, Clay, this is an area filled with drunks and hookers. Trust me, I'll get him to open that door."

"No way," Holt exclaimed. "If he even smells a trick, who knows what he might do. You're too close to things. You'll fall apart. We'll wait for the SWAT team to get here. They can handle things."

"She'll be fine." Clay spoke up for the first time. "Any talent Gracie Bryant has for acting, she got from her mother. If Libby says she can do this, then trust me, she can."

Once again Holt twisted in his seat and his gaze held Libby's for a long, breathtaking moment. "Are you sure you're up to this?"

"Positive." Libby met his gaze with a raised chin of determination.

"If you can get him to open that door without suspicion, then we can get in before he has any warning," Detective Holt replied.

The tears that only moments before had burned at her eyes dissipated as a cold calm descended on her. "I can do that," she said. She had to do it for Gracie. She would give a performance to beat all others.

They all got out of the car and quickly went over the details. Once again she tousled her hair and narrowed her eyes. As she did this she was aware of Holt, his partner and Clay moving into positions behind parked cars.

Her body trembled as she stared at the door of the motel room and took several deep, cleansing breaths. I can't do this, she thought. He'll see something in my eyes, know something isn't right. If she screwed this up something terrible might happen.

She glanced over to Clay and he nodded, his eyes filled with a calm assurance. In that nod, in his eyes, she found her strength. She was an actress and she was acting for Gracie's life.

She waited until she got the nod from Holt, then with a calm determination she staggered toward the door of

Unit 110. She knocked on the door and leaned into it. "Eddie, baby, open the door, it's me." She slurred her words in a perfect imitation of a drunk.

"There's no Eddie here. Go away," a deep voice yelled from inside the room.

"Ah, come on, baby, don't be like that. I scored us a little toot. Open up and let's party a little longer." Her heart hammered in her chest.

The door jerked open and a man peered through the crack. Blue eyes, buzz-cut blond hair and a tanned face. Libby knew in an instant that it was the man Bubbles had described who had barged into his home.

"Hey, you aren't Eddie," she exclaimed dully. "Where's Eddie?"

"I told you, you drunken bitch, that Eddie isn't..." He didn't finish the sentence as Libby was shoved sideways as Holt, his partner and Clay barreled through the open door.

"On the floor!" Holt shouted. "On the floor with your hands over your head!"

"Okay, okay! Don't shoot!" The man fell to the floor as Libby burst into the room.

A cry ripped from her as she saw her daughter lying on one of the double beds. Her eyes were closed despite the action that had just taken place in the room.

"No," the word whispered from her in an agonizing plea.

Libby's heart crashed as she realized her daughter wasn't moving.

She appeared to be dead.

Chapter 15

Clay's boots rang against the tiled floor of the dimly lit hospital corridor. It was just after ten o'clock and most of the patients and staff had settled down for the night.

The last couple of hours had flown by. The man in the motel room, Tim Cummings, had been arrested. As Holt had led him to the car, Tim had spilled his guts, telling them that Walker had orchestrated the whole thing.

Gracie had been rushed to the hospital where a blood test had confirmed that she'd been sedated, but other than that, appeared to be fine. Libby had ridden to the hospital in an ambulance with her daughter and Clay had gone with Holt to the police station to talk to Walker.

Once Holt and Clay had confronted him with their mountain of evidence, Walker had crumpled.

After listening to his confession with disgust, Clay had finally left the police station, eager to get to the hospital with the news that the bad guy was behind bars.

He nodded to the uniformed officer seated on a folding chair just outside Gracie's hospital room. Holt had provided the officer for the duration of Gracie's hospital stay.

He paused in the doorway of the room, his heart clenching at the sight that greeted him. Gracie looked tiny in the big hospital bed, but the rise and fall of her chest assured him that she slept peacefully.

Libby was in a chair, her upper body slumped on the bed as she held her daughter's hand. She was asleep, as well, and for a long moment Clay stood there and watched the two ladies who owned his heart.

Never in his life had he felt this way about any other human being. It was a feeling bigger than himself, almost too great to comprehend. It was love.

Libby started, opened her eyes and raised her head. When she saw him, the smile that curved her lips shot a piercing ache through his heart. He loved her, but his job here was done and he'd already made the decision that first thing Monday morning he'd be on a plane headed for home. Love wasn't enough to provide a happy ending for him and Libby.

He watched as Libby stood, leaned down to kiss Gracie's forehead, then joined him in the hallway just outside the room.

"Come on, let's take a walk," he said. "We could both use a cup of coffee. There's a machine in the waiting room down the hall." She frowned and looked back at her daughter. "She'll be fine," he assured her. "Officer Wilkerson here will make sure of it."

The officer nodded. "I'm not going anywhere."

Together Clay and Libby walked down the hallway to a small waiting room where there were several vending machines. "They're going to release her first thing in the morning," she said after they'd each gotten a cup of coffee. "She woke up for a few minutes a little while ago. She doesn't remember anything except that Bubbles told her he had a surprise for her. She went with him and he gave her some candy, then put her in the car."

"And that's all she remembers?" Relief flooded through him as she nodded. Thank God she didn't know the danger she'd been in. She would have no nightmares to plague her concerning the drama she'd starred in.

"What happened with Richard?"

Clay frowned. "He confessed to everything. He wrote the letters. He threw the brick through Gracie's bedroom window and he hired the fake Bubbles to kidnap her."

She leaned against the wall and shook her head. "Did he say why?"

"He did it for Kathryn. Apparently he was tired of his daughter playing second banana to Gracie the star. He figured if Gracie got out of the business then Kathryn would get the starring roles."

"Oh, my God." Libby sank down onto one of the plastic chairs the waiting room offered. She took a sip of her coffee and Clay saw in her eyes a weariness he'd never seen before.

He sat in the chair next to hers. "According to Richard, he sent the letters to terrorize you. He hoped you'd get frightened and leave the business. When that didn't work, he threw the brick and cut the rope on the set. Finally, in desperation, he came up with the kidnapping scheme."

"What was he going to do with her? He had her in the motel room, but how did he expect everything to play out?"

Clay paused and took a sip of his coffee. "He says he was just going to hold her there for a day or two, then release her."

"And do you believe him?" Her blue eyes gazed at him intently.

"To be perfectly honest with you, I don't know what to believe. I wouldn't have thought a man, a father, could be capable of such a scheme involving another child." Once again Clay realized that this world was alien to him and he never, ever, wanted it to become familiar.

"Poor Kathryn. What will happen to her now?"

"She'll live with her mother."

Libby stood, drained the coffee cup and threw it into the nearby trash. "So, it's over."

Clay stood, as well, and added his foam cup on top of hers. "It's over. Richard is going to be where he can't bother you and Gracie again for a very long time."

She nodded and then as he watched, she slowly crumpled. He grabbed her to him and held her tight as she cried what he knew were tears of relief.

He closed his eyes as she molded her body to his. He drew deep breaths, memorizing the feel of her curves

against him, the scent of her. He wanted to remember everything about the way she felt in his arms, for he knew
that this would be the last time he'd ever hold her.

Today is the day Clay's leaving.

This was the first thought Libby had when she opened
her eyes Monday morning. She rolled over onto her back
and stared up to where the early morning sun shot golden
shards of light across the ceiling.

She should be elated. The danger was over. Gracie
would go back to work today to complete the filming of
the movie and life was back to normal. But somehow
normal felt different than it had before Clay had arrived
with his sexy smile and hot desire.

And today he was leaving.

The depression that whispered at the edge of her brain
troubled her. She shouldn't be depressed. She'd known all
along that Clay was here to do a job and now that job was
over.

What they needed was routine…work. It was time to
get up, get busy and by this time tomorrow Clay West
would be nothing more than a distant memory.

By the time she showered and dressed for the day she'd
managed to shove the depression deep into the recesses of
her mind. She had things to do, decisions to make. The
movie should be in the can by the end of the week and she
needed to figure out what project came next.

She had three firm offers for Gracie on her desk, offers
that had come in over the past week while Gracie had been

recuperating with her twisted ankle. One of the offers was the script Jordan had discussed with her days earlier. It was for a movie being shot on location in Wyoming and there was a part of Libby. She thought it might be good for them to get out of town, get away from everything and enjoy something new and different.

As she made her way down the stairs and toward the kitchen she braced herself to see Clay, but was surprised to discover that he wasn't in his usual place drinking coffee at the small kitchen table.

"I'm the first one down?" she asked Helen.

"Haven't seen hide nor hair of him this morning," she replied. "Breakfast will be ready in ten minutes."

"Thank you, Helen." Libby drifted from the kitchen and into the dining room. She'd awakened Gracie, who should be down soon. They'd eat breakfast, the car would arrive and they'd tell Clay a final goodbye. Then it would be life back to usual.

She'd just sat at the table when Gracie came bounding into the room. Her heart exploded with joy as she saw Gracie's carefree smile, the blue eyes that displayed no shadows, no haunting from her ordeal.

"Where's Mr. Clay? We can't eat breakfast without him," she said as she slid into her seat at the table.

"Here I am." The deep voice came from the doorway and despite her best intentions to stay disconnected from him, a small shiver went up Libby's spine.

He looked much as he had the first day he'd arrived. Clad in his jeans and a short-sleeved shirt, he dropped his suitcase just outside the dining room door, then slid into his chair at the table.

Before he could say anything else Helen began to serve their breakfast. Thankfully, Gracie was her usual, bubbly self, chattering about the upcoming week, the fun she had at the birthday party and how nice the nurses had been in her brief stay in the hospital.

Libby was grateful for her daughter's chatter because for the first time since Clay had arrived in her home, she didn't know what to say to him. What horrified her even more was that she couldn't imagine telling him goodbye.

All too soon breakfast was over and the car had arrived. Clay picked up his suitcase and walked with them to the front door.

"We could give you a ride to the airport," Libby said as they stepped out the front door. The lump of emotion that suddenly filled her throat surprised her.

"I've already called for a taxi. It should be arriving at any moment."

"Mr. Clay, I don't want you to go to the airport. I want you to come to the studio with us." Gracie looked up at him, her eyes huge.

"Remember, honey. I told you yesterday that Mr. Clay had to go home today," Libby said gently.

Gracie's lower lip quivered. "But I don't want him to go home."

Clay fell to one knee in front of Gracie. He looked at her with such love that Libby's heart twisted painfully. This was going to be much harder than she'd anticipated.

"Honey, it's time for me to go back to my house and see my horses and pick carrots out of Mr. Red's garden." His voice seemed deeper, thicker than usual.

Tears splashed down Gracie's cheeks and she threw her arms around his neck. "These are real tears, not pretend," she said. "And I don't want you to go because I love you too much."

Clay closed his eyes and hugged her tight. Libby watched and felt the press of her own tears. Damn him. Damn him for making her daughter love him.

"I love you, too," Clay whispered, then released her and stood. "You run on to the car. I need to talk to your mom for a minute."

Gracie did as he told her. When she was in the backseat, Clay turned to Libby. He stared at her for a long moment, then looked back toward the car.

"You asked me that first night that we made love if I'd ever felt passionate about anything in my life and I told you I hadn't. If you asked me that same question right now, I'd have a different answer for you."

He looked back at her again and his green eyes held a wealth of emotion, emotion that caused Libby's heart to beat just a little faster. "I feel passionate about Gracie, but I feel even more passionate about you." He swiped a hand through his hair, looking as if he'd rather be anywhere but standing in front of her.

"I love you, Libby. I never expected it, I sure as hell don't like it, but there it is. I love you and I just wanted you to know. And there's something else I want you to know.

Whether your parents knew it or not, whether you're acting or the mother of an actress or just plain breathing, you're special."

Her chest constricted and she felt the press of tears at his words. He loved her. "Clay…" She said his name but had no idea how to follow it.

He held up a hand to still her, his features radiating a painful reality. "I love you, Libby, but we both know it's not going anywhere. We have different wants, different needs." Anything else he might have said was cut off as a taxi pulled up to the gate and honked.

"That's my ride." He leaned forward and kissed her cheek, a soft, lingering kiss that scorched her to her core. "If you ever decide this place, this work, isn't what you really want, what you really need, you can always find me at the West place in Cotter Creek." He plopped his cowboy hat on his head.

With her heart in her throat she watched him as he walked down the driveway toward the awaiting taxi. It was only when the taxi pulled away that tears splashed down her cheeks.

Real tears, not pretend.

"Charlie, I told you I haven't made a decision yet. Believe me, you'll be the first one to know when I've decided." Libby disconnected the call and leaned back in her desk chair.

A headache pounded at her temples and she rubbed her fingers on the sides of her head in an attempt to alleviate the pressure.

Gracie's movie had wrapped up two days ago and Charlie had been pressuring her to make a decision about what happened next for Gracie.

For the first time in as long as she could remember, Libby was indecisive. Nothing felt right for Gracie. Maybe they needed a little vacation from work, a hiatus of sorts. They could go to the beach for a couple of weeks, or to the mountains.

She stood and massaged the back of her neck. Clay. Thoughts of him jumped into her head as they had during the past week, unbidden and painful.

Even though he was gone, he was still present in her heart. Each and every moment they had shared was carved into her soul. Everything he had said to her had played and replayed in her mind.

She moved to the window and peered out at the perfectly manicured lawn that spoke of success. And waited for the burst of pride, the feeling of pleasure that should have accompanied it.

Nothing.

For the past week she'd felt nothing.

Had Clay been right? Had she been trying to fulfill childhood needs through Gracie? Had she mistakenly believed this dream of stardom had been Gracie's when all along it had been nothing more than the wistful want of the lonely child she had been?

She dropped her hand from her neck with a sigh of exasperation. If she let her mind wander down that road, she'd go crazy. Clay was gone and life went on.

What she needed at the moment was a cup of hot tea. That never failed to ease a tension headache. She left her office and went into the kitchen where Helen was busy preparing the evening meal.

"I won't get in your way," she said to the older woman. "I just want to get a cup of hot tea."

"Sit," Helen instructed, and pointed to the table. "I'll get it for you." Libby shot her a grateful smile and sank down at the table.

"Doesn't quite seem the same around here, does it? Without that man hanging around." Helen put a cup of water in the microwave to heat.

"No, it doesn't," Libby agreed softly. Whenever she thought of Clay telling her that he loved her, it hurt.

Helen fixed the tea and placed it on the table in front of Libby, then sat on the chair facing her. "I thought maybe you and he had something good together."

"We did, but he's not a Hollywood kind of man," Libby said.

"Hollywood, it's a town that eats its young," Helen said with unusual passion. Libby looked at her in surprise. Helen stared down at the tabletop, then looked up at Libby and in the older woman's eyes Libby saw grief. "I had a daughter, you know."

"No, I didn't know," Libby said.

"She was an actress. She never made it big like Gracie, but she worked all the time. Danielle was her name. It was just her and me, like it is with you and Gracie. Danielle worked steady until she turned about thirteen."

Libby wasn't sure she wanted to hear this. She heard Helen's pain in the words and knew the story didn't have a happy ending.

"About that time Danielle went from cute as a button to gangly and awkward. You know that stage, all arms and legs and feet too big for their bodies. Anyway, the offers dried up and Danielle didn't know how to be anything else but an actress. She was frantic and depressed, and when she was fifteen she died from a drug overdose."

Libby gasped. "Helen, I'm so sorry. I didn't know…"

"It's not something I dwell on. It happened a long time ago. I would have never told you, but Gracie is such a sweet little girl. I just want you to know that both success and failure in this business sometimes creates the same bad things. Make sure this is really what you want for her, because it's not an easy life like some people think."

Libby's headache pounded more painfully. First Clay, now Helen. She knew the pitfalls of this business as well as anyone.

No matter what Helen thought, no matter what Clay had said to her, she told herself once again that she was merely being a good mother and making certain that Gracie got the opportunities to follow her dreams.

Chapter 16

Clay stood at the window in the dining room of his father's large ranch house, staring at the landscape he loved. White-faced beef cattle grazed in the distance on the lush green grass and an explosion of wildflowers colored the hillside.

If the window had been open he would have smelled the welcoming scents of cattle and earth, of sweet grass and sunshine. He loved this place, this land, and felt more centered here than anyplace else.

"You going to stare out that window all night or are you going to sit down for supper?" His father's voice came from behind him.

He turned to see Red and Smokey seated at the table, waiting for him. "Sorry." He quickly took his seat at the long oak table. "I'm thinking about buying the Butler house in town," Clay announced.

Red looked at him in surprise. "What brought this on? You know you always have a place here."

Clay nodded. "I know that. I just think it's time for me to put down some roots of my own."

"If Sheila Wadsworth is the Realtor, then the price is probably ridiculously high," Smokey exclaimed, and scowled. "That woman thinks she's Donald Trump."

Clay smiled. "I'll make an offer and either she accepts it or rejects it."

He wasn't sure what had prompted the decision to buy a place of his own. He told himself it was just time and he planned on taking some time off and to use that time to get settled into his own place. But, deep inside, he thought it was prompted by the fact that for a brief period of time he'd gotten an idea of what it would be like to have family, to have a wife and a daughter.

As always whenever thoughts of Libby and Gracie crossed his mind a stabbing pain accompanied them. Even though it had been a little more than a week since he'd left Hollywood and Libby and Gracie behind, his pain at this moment was as great as when he'd walked down the driveway to get into the taxi to leave.

After dinner he decided to take a sunset ride on Amos. The horse greeted him with a friendly nuzzle and stood patiently as Clay saddled him up for a ride.

Within minutes Clay and Amos were flying across the pasture. They passed Tanner's house, which had been rebuilt after a fire. As he went by he saw Tanner's wife, Anna, on the porch. She waved, her blond hair sparkling in the evening sun.

That flash of blond hair brought back thoughts of Libby. It was hell, loving somebody who didn't have the capacity to love you back. He figured he'd gotten as close to Libby as anyone ever had, but apparently his love hadn't been enough for her.

He drew in a deep breath, enjoying the sweet scent of the grass, the rich odor of the Oklahoma dirt and the fragrance of the wildflowers that dotted the pasture. It smelled like home.

Had he been the one who had made a mistake? Had he been selfish in wanting it to be his way or no way? Maybe, but he'd known that Libby wasn't the kind of woman to compromise what she believed in, what she wanted, for anyone. She was a Hollywood woman. He was an Oklahoma man.

Besides, he'd never be able to be with her and support the decisions she made for Gracie. Right or wrong, he couldn't set aside his feelings about Gracie's career.

The sun had kissed the horizon when he headed back toward the house. He'd hoped the ride would clear his mind, give him some peace, but it had done neither.

He'd just arrived at the stable when he saw the approach of a car in the distance. Dust devils rose up as it came closer and closer.

He got off Amos and handed the reins to a ranch hand, then looked to see the car turning into the entrance to the ranch.

It was a silver car, one he'd never seen before. Joshua? His brother was expected to return home in the next couple of weeks, but it would be just like him to appear unannounced.

It wasn't until he noticed there were two people in the car and the sun glinted off the blond hair of the driver that his heartbeat went wild.

Almost before the car came to a complete stop, the passenger door opened and Gracie flew out. "Mr. Clay! We came to your home." She ran to his awaiting arms and he grabbed her up and held her tight. She smelled like bubble gum and innocence and love.

"I'm so happy to see you," he said, then his gaze went to Libby who had gotten out of the driver's seat.

"I'm so happy to see you," Gracie exclaimed. "I missed you so much."

Clay held his emotions in check, afraid to hope, afraid to guess what their arrival here meant. He carried Gracie over to where Libby stood hesitantly at the side of the car.

"Hi," he said, his gaze drinking her in.

"Surprised?"

"Very." He set Gracie on the ground as his father and Smokey stepped out onto the front porch. "Come on in."

When they reached the porch, Clay made the introductions. Gracie looked at Smokey with curious eyes. "Are you cranky?"

Smokey raised his grizzled eyebrows in surprise. "Only with people who are aggravating."

"Am I aggravating?" she asked.

A glint of humor touched Smokey's eyes. "Not yet."

"Good." She directed her attention to Red. "Mr. Red, would you show me your garden? Mr. Clay told me you have the best garden in the whole wide world."

"I'd be happy to show you my garden," Red agreed with a smile. "Come on, honey." Together Red and Gracie walked off the porch and headed around the house.

"I'll go put on some coffee," Smokey said, and disappeared into the house, leaving Libby and Clay alone on the front porch.

Clay wanted to ask her a million questions. He wanted to take her into his arms and kiss her until he could kiss her no longer. Instead he waited for her to speak, for her to explain exactly what she and Gracie were doing here.

"I've spent the last week thinking," she said, and leaned against the porch railing. "I've been thinking about my life, thinking about Gracie's. I've been thinking about where I've been and where we're going."

"That's a lot of thinking."

She smiled then, that smile that made him feel as if everything in the world was all right. "Yes, it is."

He jammed his hands into his pockets to keep them from reaching for her. "And did you come to some conclusions during all that thinking time?"

"I came to the conclusion that a lot of what you said to me the night we had that awful fight was true." Her smile fell away and instead a tiny frown appeared in the center of her forehead.

"I did believe that I was doing what was best for Gracie,

that I was being the kind of mother I'd never had, supporting my daughter in her dreams. But you were right. Gracie has no real dreams of her own. I was wishing my dream onto her."

"Libby, I had no right to say those things to you."

"Loving Gracie gave you the right." She worried a hand through her hair and looked out across the expanse of land. "It's as beautiful here as I imagined."

"Libby, what are you doing here?" He could stand it no longer. He had to know.

"Yesterday I asked Gracie if she was ready to start making a new movie. You know how she answered me? She said okay, if that's what I wanted her to do. Then I asked her if she'd like to take some time off and once again she said that would be fine if that's what I wanted. I realized then that Gracie doesn't have the same kind of driving need that I had as a child. The only need she has is to make me happy."

She shoved away from the railing and began to pace. Clay tamped down a bit of frustration, knowing that there was no way to hurry Libby. She did and would always do things in her own way, in her own time.

She stopped pacing and looked at him once again. "Did you know that Helen had a daughter who was an actress? She died of a drug overdose when she was fifteen years old."

That explained the feeling Clay had gotten that there was more to the old woman than met the eye. "But a lot of kids work in Hollywood and grow up to be healthy, happy, well-adjusted adults," he said, wondering why in the hell he was playing devil's advocate. "And if anyone had a chance of being well-adjusted it would be Gracie, because she has a loving mother like you."

She cast him a grateful smile that held for a moment then fell away once again. "You asked me why we're here. We're here because I realized I'd built my life around Gracie, that without her I had nothing of my own. We're here because Richard frightened me and made me realize the risks that are inherent in the business I chose for my daughter."

She took two steps forward, coming to stand so close in front of him that he could smell her scent, feel her heat. "But more than anything we're here because I love you, Clay. I love you like I've never loved any man before. We're here because I've only found one place where I feel special, where I feel loved, and that place is in your arms."

Her words filled him with a welcoming heat, with a joy the likes of which he'd never known before. He pulled her to him and kissed her with all the love that beat in his heart.

She returned his kiss, her arms twining around his neck as her heart beat frantically against his. Even though Clay had been home for a week, this was the first time he felt as if he truly was home.

When the kiss ended she leaned against him and once again stared out at the Oklahoma landscape. "You aren't in Hollywood anymore," he said.

She smiled up at him, her eyes as pure and blue as the Oklahoma sky. "You make that sound like it's a bad thing."

He gazed at her intently. "Can it be enough for you, Libby?"

She placed a loving hand on the side of his face. "You're enough for me." He kissed her once again and tasted his future in her lips.

"Mommy!"

Clay and Libby sprang apart at the sound of Gracie's voice. She stood by the side of the house, plump red tomatoes clutched in her hand. Red stood next to her, grinning at the couple on the porch.

"Mommy, I saw you. You were kissing Mr. Clay! Does that mean you're going to marry him and he'll be my very own daddy?"

Clay waited for Libby's reply. "I don't know," Libby said. "Mr. Clay hasn't asked me to marry him yet."

"Marry me, Libby," he said urgently, with all the need for her that was in his soul. "Say you'll marry me."

"We say yes!" Gracie exclaimed. She smiled up at Red. "We say yes, yes, yes! And that means Mr. Clay is my daddy and you're my grandpa Red. This is the very best day of my life!"

"This is the best day of my life," Libby repeated, and smiled up at Clay, her blue eyes filled with love.

"Oh, honey, this is just the beginning," he murmured, awed by the fact that his job of guarding Gracie had become the joy of loving Libby.

* * * * *

**Hidden in the secrets of antiquity,
lies the unimagined truth...**

Introducing

a brand-new line filled with mystery
and suspense, action and adventure,
and a fascinating look into history.

And it all begins with DESTINY.

In a sealed crypt in
France, where the
terrifying legend of
the beast of Gevaudan
begins to unravel,
Annja Creed discovers
a stunning artifact
that will seal her destiny.

*Available every other
month starting
July 2006, wherever
you buy books.*

BOMBSHELL™

A LOST HISTORY COMES TO LIGHT.

The Madonna Key

Don't miss a single installment of
THE MADONNA KEY, a new Silhouette Bombshell
miniseries beginning July 2006.

Silhouette BOMBSHELL

$1.00 OFF

A LOST HISTORY COMES TO LIGHT.

The Madonna Key

Don't miss a single installment of
THE MADONNA KEY, a new Silhouette Bombshell
miniseries beginning July 2006.

Pick up *Lost Calling* by Evelyn Vaughn,
or any other July adventure from
Silhouette Bombshell and receive

$1.00 OFF

Coupon expires September 30, 2006.
Redeemable at participating retail outlets in
Canada only. Limit one coupon per customer.

52606872